BACK TO THE HIGHLANDS

LOVE THROUGHOUT TIME
BOOK FOUR

ID JOHNSON

Copyright © 2025 by ID Johnson

All rights reserved.

No part of this book may be reproduced in any form or by any electronic or mechanical means, including information storage and retrieval systems, without written permission from the author, except for the use of brief quotations in a book review.

Cover by Sparrow Book Cover Designs

For submissions to Rogue Wolf Publishing, please see our website: www.roguewolfpublishing.com. No agent necessary.

For Mr. Richards

CONTENTS

Chapter 1   1
Chapter 2   7
Chapter 3   13
Chapter 4   19
Chapter 5   25
Chapter 6   31
Chapter 7   37
Chapter 8   43
Chapter 9   49
Chapter 10   55
Chapter 11   61
Chapter 12   67
Chapter 13   73
Chapter 14   77
Chapter 15   83
Chapter 16   89
Chapter 17   95
Chapter 18   101
Chapter 19   107
Chapter 20   113
Chapter 21   119
Chapter 22   125
Chapter 23   133
Chapter 24   141
Chapter 25   151
Chapter 26   157
Chapter 27   163
Chapter 28   171
Chapter 29   177
Chapter 30   185
Chapter 31   191

Also by ID Johnson   195

CHAPTER 1

The wrap party has all the elements of a medieval victory banquet. Velvet banners in ruby and gold, torches flickering in their iron brackets, and the clink of goblets overflowing with ale.

Tonight, we celebrate the milestone of shooting the final cinematic scene, and I marvel at the chance to party in a real Scottish medieval castle.

This ancient building represents the contrast between luxurious elegance and primitivity. Massive wooden beams support the ceilings while rich, colorful, tapestries proudly displayed on the stone walls depict battles fought in another time.

Everyone is dressed as we were on the set of *Where the River Runs Crimson*, in 16th-century Highlander apparel. The plot is based on the life of a warrior who had to choose between fighting in battle or staying and defending his wife and many children from rival rogue clansmen who were wreaking havoc on people's farms.

The actors wear their costumes effortlessly, having spent much more time in such attire than the producers and crew. Even the waiters and staff are dressed in period garb.

I grab a goblet and mingle. The people I've met and the friendships I've made while working on this project have been great. Tonight will be the last time I'll be seeing many of them for a while since my job here is done and my heartstrings are tugged at the thought.

Approaching a group of actors I taught how to shoot a longbow, I half-listen to their conversation while gazing up at the cathedral ceilings of the ballroom, and think I would have enjoyed living in such a beautiful and massive place, five hundred years ago.

Looking down at my red and black plaid belted doublet with brass buttons, a black sporran at my waist, and matching leather boots, I certainly would have looked the part.

"You are dressed like a rich dude tonight," Max, who plays the role of a Scottish warrior, teases, and the others chime in with laughter.

I blush and jovially reply, "Thanks, Max. I'll remember you next time I'm in need of fashion advice."

Max is giving me a hard time because most of the last six months I spent wearing ancient Highlander battle gear, and tonight I look less muddy and bloody.

"We kid you because we like you, Rory," Eve says. She is the leading lady in the film.

"Yes, and you really do clean up well. I mean, look at these nobleman-looking threads!" Max agrees.

"To Rory Graham," he proposes a toast, and everyone raises their drink. "The best battle instructor we've ever had!"

Goblets clink, and as I point out, "That's because I'm the only battle instructor you've ever had." Laughter erupts.

I glance around at their beaming faces, surprised by a toast in my honor. Usually, I'm behind the scenes, so being the center of attention —even if just temporarily— feels good. I savor the moment, sipping slowly.

As the conversation shifts, I let my eyes wander. The night is still young, so I excuse myself and continue exploring the room.

Highland fifers and fiddlers play in one corner while extras from the film, still in costume, listen and dance with champagne flutes in hand.

On the opposite side of the room from the musicians are tables with incredible-smelling food. My nose and growling stomach pull me over to take a peek at the display. A roasted boar, venison pies, and heaping bowls of berries are the perfect combination of extravagant and authentic.

"Well, don't you look handsome in that getup?" Fiona slides up next to me while I make a plate of food.

"Thank you." I wink. "But you don't prefer the battle kilt slathered in fake blood and real mud?"

"We historians prefer scrolls and dates over gore." Fiona giggles and takes a sip of red wine.

"Yeah, you get scrolls and dates. I get bruises and superficial wounds," I reply, and we both laugh.

Ours was an easy friendship, and I'm going to miss seeing Fiona every day. She was a historian on the film, and I, a former Navy SEAL with a penchant for obscure historical trivia, was the combat expert and trainer. On this film, fencing, archery, and intense hand-to-hand combat scenes had us working together sometimes until dawn.

Fiona and I bonded quickly over endless takes reworking fight scenes. Her positivity, patience, and sense of humor kept everyone going most nights.

"I'll miss working with you," I say, smiling.

"I'll miss my American friend too," she says, stealing a strawberry from my plate. "Who knows? Our paths might cross one day. We might get to work together again. But for now, come on." She tugs on my sleeve.

Fiona's eyes are shimmering with mischief, and I know that if I follow her tonight, I'll have a blast.

"Come on where?" I ask, feigning concern.

"Just come on." She slips her arm under mine and pulls me through the crowd.

Chuckling, I set my plate on a table and let her lead me out of the castle doors.

"Do you ever think about what it must have been like to live here back then? All the pain, glory, blood, and heartache?" Fiona asks, swaying slightly, the moonlight blanketing her pretty face.

Noticing Fiona might be a tad tipsy, I reply, "I do think about it, all the time."

After many long nights on set, I've noticed the way she becomes more animated with each glass of wine. Her eyes sparkle brighter, her words more colorful, and the enthusiasm in her voice is impossible to ignore. There's something undeniably charming about how she talks about history when she's tipsy.

"Tell me more," I coax her, leaning in. "Scottish history has always interested me. I might be from Tennessee, but my family's lineage is from your country."

"Oh, you told me." Fiona chuckles. "You told me many times, my friend. Well, do you want to know about the brave people who lived here?" she asks as we stroll the castle grounds. I nod, and she leads the way down a path into the forest.

"The MacRae clan held these lands in the mid-1500s. Laird and Lady MacRae and their son and daughter. Times were peaceful and things were going well until some greedy people came from the south. Rival clans wanting to add MacRae land to their own." Good lore sounds better coated in her accent.

"So what happened?" I ask. Fiona's stories are always enthralling. Maybe it's the twinkle in her eye or her Scottish lilt.

She faces me, walking backward on unsteady feet. The low, powerful growl of the roaring river gets louder as we draw nearer, and Fiona has to speak up. "They were ambushed. Several times. They rallied their troops and ally clans over and over again, defending their land at all costs."

I want to hear the rest of Fiona's story, but I'm distracted by an old wooden plank bridge dangling across a rushing river behind her.

Fiona goes on with her tale as I try to decide if we are too buzzed to attempt the bridge. "Laird and Lady MacRae's son and daughter were warriors who fought valiantly for their people and their land," Fiona says, turning away from me to step onto the first piece of rotting bridge wood.

"As much as I want to hear the end of the story and find out if the MacRae clan won, I don't trust this bridge, Fiona. It is almost in the water, it's so low, and it looks like it's as old as this legend." I reach for her to pull her back toward me on the river bank.

"Their bridge back then probably looked just like this one, you're right about that! But where's your sense of adventure, Rory Graham?!" She impishly taunts me, and although I am wary of the bridge, I'm even more attracted to Fiona's magically enticing voice.

She pulls me by the hand onto rickety planks, and I feel a rush of adrenaline. The fragile bridge is swaying in the breeze and the water beneath us is moving fast.

A strong gust of wind catches a lock of Fiona's dark hair, tossing it around as though Mother Nature is flirting with her. Crackles of lightning brighten the sky, momentarily casting her face in a soft glowing light.

"Are you some sort of Gaelic witch?" I jest. "It's not supposed to rain, and yet every time you tell a fairy tale, something unexpectedly spooky happens to add to the ambiance."

Fiona throws her head back in a silly witch cackle and says, "Oh, just because the armor in the costume room started to move on its own when I was telling a story about a battle, everyone thinks I'm a witch."

I laugh at the memory. Several times, Fiona began to tell the cast and crew a little-known historical fact, and the armor would crash to the floor for no apparent reason. Funny coincidences made working with her enchanting, and everyone teased her about being witchy.

Thunder rumbles, and rain begins to fall.

"Besides, this is not a fairy tale, Rory!" She smacks my arm playfully. "It's true!"

The wind picks up, as does the rain, and Fiona's face tightens with fear. I read her lips: "Let's go!"

We turn back across the bridge to the bank, and from behind, I hear Fiona scream. I spin around just in time to see her splash into the river.

Immediately, I dive in after her. The churning river crashes against us, its force driving Fiona into me as the current tugs at my limbs. I pull her head above water, and she gasps for air.

Supporting her body weight on my right shoulder, I feel her cough up water. Though I'm relieved she's breathing, I know we are too far from the bank to swim in these conditions. I let the water move us back toward the bridge.

Reaching above my head, I grab the bridge with one hand and help Fiona up on it with the other.

Holding onto the bridge as tightly as I can, I begin to climb up just as Fiona had. She screams to me, "You can do it, Rory! Pull yourself up!"

But the rope is too slippery, and the current is too strong. I lose my grip, and the river swallows me whole.

CHAPTER 2

CAIT

I came outside for fresh air, but the breeze is heavy tonight, suffocating. I can feel the weight of my father's words pressing on my chest. "Cait, I have chosen Lachlan."

I can't bear those words, let alone the thought of marrying Lachlan. My betrothal looms like a storm cloud, dark and ominous, and no matter how much I long for freedom, it is not mine to claim.

I want to be my own woman, free to wield a sword, to fight for my clan, and not be shackled to a life of dullness and silence as a wife. Worse still, Lachlan stirs a cold unease within me. I don't trust him, and there's a shadow behind his smile that makes my skin crawl. The thought of being bound to him tightens like a noose around my throat.

I needed to escape the castle walls, entirely. The whispers of the servants, the sharp glances of my mother as she frets over every detail of the wedding, smother me. A never-ending parade of gowns and menu options. The details are unavoidable, and the oppression of tradition presses down on me like a boulder.

So I stole away a moment to myself in the woods, seeking respite from the disappointment of my father's words and the ever-present eyes of my family.

My boots crunch against the earth, each step a small rebellion. I am the daughter of Laird MacRae, yet tonight, I am no one. No noblewoman. No betrothed. Just a girl seeking breath, seeking solace in the wild.

Just Cait.

The river races, its surface surging milky white in the moonlight. I lean against a rough tree trunk and stare down into the current. There is something about the chaos of the river that calms me. Her utter refusal to be tamed by the hands of men. I imagine she is ferine, carefree, unburdened by tradition.

I close my eyes, just for a moment, letting the peace of the night wash over me. But the tranquility is shattered, abrupt and jarring, by a sudden splash.

A body breaks through the water's surface, flailing, limbs thrashing against the water. Panic rises in my chest, a flash of fear seizing me before I steady myself. I rush to the river's edge, my pulse quickening. Whoever fell in is struggling, the river pulling them down.

I don't hesitate. The rope lies coiled about the bridge post, meant for times such as this. I hurry over and seize it, casting one end toward them with haste.

"Hold fast!" I call out.

A hand reaches up, fingers grasping at the rope. When I feel their body weight and am sure they have a hold, I pull with all my strength.

The river is unforgiving, its torrent relentless. I refuse to let go. I slip the toes of my boots under a thick tree root to keep from sliding in the mud. I'm desperate to pull this soul from the water before they drown.

I haul a limp, unsteady body partway up the bank, and it is only then that I see that he is a man. He gathers himself enough to climb the rest of the way up, out of the water.

His muscles strain beneath the wet fabric. Broad shoulders, strong arms, every line of him built for this kind of fight. It's clear he's in powerful condition, otherwise, the river would've kept him.

He gasps for air, and I back away, trying to catch my breath as well. I study his appearance in the faint glow of the moonlight. His clothing, rich and elegant, clings to his form, soaking wet. Clearly, he is a noble man, but his build appears to be that of a worker or a warrior. He has dark hair, a strong jaw, and a handsome face that is unfamiliar.

"Fiona? Are you okay?" he mutters, his voice rough, confused.

Fiona? Okay?

I take a few more steps back, my heart racing with uncertainty. His voice and words do not match the language of my people. His accent is strange, like nothing I've ever heard before. He stares at me, blinking slowly.

"Eh...?" I put my hand on my dagger, wary. All of my instincts warn me to be cautious. The clans are restless. Rivalries run deep. And this man, this stranger, could be from a rival clan.

His gaze locks on mine, and he shakes his head as if trying to clear it.

"Where is Fiona?" he asks, his words slow, thick with bewilderment. His eyes narrow, and for a moment, I think he might be winedrunk. Slowly lifting himself from the wet ground, he seems to be in a stupor, dazed.

"Who are you? Where did you come from?" I ask, my voice trembling.

He looks at me again, his lips parting slightly. Then, as though remembering something, he shakes his head. "I'm not sure what's going on here, but you're not who I thought *you* were."

I take a step toward him, feeling the pull of curiosity. "Who did you think I was?"

He stares at me, his face clouded with uncertainty. "Fiona. I thought... you were my friend Fiona...." He trails off.

"I am Cait MacRae," I say, trying to keep my voice steady. "Daughter of Laird MacRae. And you, stranger, are not from these lands, are you?"

His dismay deepens, his eyes searching my face. "MacRae?" He says as though it's a question, his brows furrowing in a way that tells me he doesn't understand. "I—"

"Where do you come from?" I cut him off, strengthening my tone. "Speak plainly. You are not from the clans! Who are you?"

"Rory. Rory Graham…."

He exhales sharply, and there is a flicker of intensity in his eyes. He blinks and glances around, taking in the dark forest that surrounds us.

The wind picks up, rustling the leaves, and then his gaze shifts back to me.

"I'm… I'm from…." He falters again, then looks up at me with an expression of sheer frustration. "I don't understand. I was—I was somewhere else. And now…." He gestures helplessly around him.

"Somewhere else?" I repeat, doubtful. "You're lost. And you're not a member of the McRae clan."

"I… I'm no… not quite a clan member." He scratches his head.

A chill skitters down my spine. He's telling the truth, or at least, I think he is. I can see it in his eyes. His words, though strange, are not threats. Maybe he hit his head when he fell into the river and really can't remember.

How did I miss him on the bridge before he fell?

The wind picks up again, biting at my skin, and I shiver. "I should get you to shelter. Come, let's get you out of these wet clothes."

But he shakes his head. "No, I…." He blinks rapidly. "I need to understand. What happened?"

I hesitate, still unsure of him, yet something in me compels me to help. He seems so genuinely puzzled, I almost let down my guard.

"You are lost," I say, softer now. "But you are unharmed. For now."

I shall aid him. Indeed, what other choice remains? Though a stranger, he stands in need of succor on MacRae land.

I look him over carefully. "Walk ahead of me," I say, my voice low, yet bold. "I'll guide you. It's best I keep my eyes on you as we go."

My gaze never falters, the warning clear beneath my words: I trust him no more than the night itself—so he knows better than to try anything clever.

The forest path twists and climbs, guiding us toward the looming silhouette of my home. Its stone walls press against the starlit sky, a familiar sanctuary, sharply contrasting the swirling confusion of everything that has just transpired.

I hear the stranger muttering softly under his breath, words tangled in an accent challenging to my ears, but I say nothing. He is difficult to understand, not only in tongue, but in demeanor. Although, there's something endearing in his perplexity, and it only deepens the mystery that clings to him like the dampness of his clothes.

At last, the castle gates come into view. He stops just short of the threshold. Turning to face me, he asks, "This… this is where you live?"

"Aye," I answer proudly.

He looks at me with a mixture of hesitation and disbelief. Even in his unease, there is a rugged handsomeness to him. Moreover, how can a nobleman be so hale and strong, as though forged for battle rather than courtly ease?

Without knowing who he is, and if he has hit his head or is lost to the ale, on my land, I am bound to protect him.

He places his trust in my hospitality, and we step through the gates together.

CHAPTER 3

Rory

The castle looms against the night sky, dark and intimidating, its towers outlined in silver moonlight. I stop just short of the gate, staring up. I know this place. I stood in this very spot hours ago, or what feels like hours ago. Only then it was lit by floodlights and filled with partygoers in costumes.

"This... this is your home?" I ask, breath fogging the air.

"Aye," Cait says, stepping past me and lifting a hand to the guards above the gate. "Open the gate!"

Her voice is strong and commanding.

The massive wooden gates creak open. I expect some kind of joke, a hidden camera, a drone buzzing overhead, something to shatter this illusion. But it never comes. Just the groan of heavy hinges and the scrape of boots on packed dirt as guards close the massive gate behind us.

Cait gestures for me to follow, and I do, because what other choice do I have?

The courtyard is dimly lit by a few torches. There are no street-lights, no headlights, and no cars parked nearby. My heart pounds harder.

"I'll introduce you to my family," Cait says as we cross beneath a stone archway. "My father will want to know who you are."

Panic flashes through me. *Who am I? Everyone at the party knew who I was... who should I say I am now?*

"Who is your father?" I ask apologetically.

She glances at me over her shoulder. "Laird MacRae."

Of course. Laird MacRae... because I've fallen into *Braveheart*.

"I'm not sure that's a good idea," I say. My voice cracks, unsteady. "Maybe I could just dry off somewhere. Quietly."

But she's already pushing open the enormous wooden door. "My father must be told of all who set foot on his land," she says, pausing to meet my eyes. "No one enters MacRae ground without his knowledge."

The film I worked on taught me enough about 16th-century hospitality to know that strangers didn't just *drop in* without raising suspicion. I wipe water from my face, trying not to look like a total lunatic. But I feel like one. Everything is spinning.

Inside, it's warmer. A fire blazes in the hearth of a long stone hall. The walls are hung with tapestries–actual tapestries, not replicas, their worn threads and faded colors telling stories only time could weave. There's the clink of metal, the murmur of voices. And then footsteps.

A tall man with graying hair and a presence as commanding as thunder appears at the far end of the hall. He's wrapped in a plaid cloak, and beside him stands a woman, stern, elegant, eyes sharp enough to cut.

"Mother. Father," Cait says, tilting her head in a formal bow. "This man was found in the river. He nearly drowned."

They both look at me like I might explode.

I try to speak, to explain myself, but what comes out is a dry, "A pleasure to meet you."

Their expressions do not soften.

"Whence do you hail?" the woman asks, her gaze shifting from stern to unsettled.

"He says his name is Rory Graham," Cait answers for me, clearly omitting the part where it was she who rescued me. "He's… lost."

"A foreigner," her father says, frowning. "He speaks oddly."

"English, I think," Cait adds. "Though not like any I've heard."

"I'm from—" I start, then cut myself off.

Not Tennessee.

"Uhm, I'm from the south," I finish lamely.

A younger man appears in the doorway. Mid-twenties, maybe. His shoulders are broad, and he is a bit taller than Laird MacRae. He eyes me with open curiosity.

Lady MacRae narrows her eyes. "You look like a man accustomed to comfort, yet you've the build of a soldier."

I can't tell if that's suspicion or approval.

"I've had… an unusual journey," I say.

Cait's father grunts. "You'll speak more of it in time. For now, Duncan will see you to dry clothes."

"This is my brother, Duncan," Cait says. "He'll show you to a guest chamber."

"Come on, then," Duncan says, waving me forward.

I glance back at Cait before I follow, but she has already turned in the opposite direction.

I follow Duncan down a narrow hallway, lit by flickering torches. He doesn't speak for a while, just walks ahead, and I trail behind like a kid on a school tour, trying not to gawk.

"You hail from the south?" Duncan asks, glancing back.

"Yes, or, uhm, aye," I reply, my voice echoing too loudly.

He opens a door revealing a chamber with a small fireplace, bed, and a low table. A wool tunic and trousers lie folded across a bench.

"I'll send for someone to dry your clothes," Duncan says, placing a candle on the table.

As he lights the fire, I nod numbly. "Thank you."

He pauses at the door, studying me again. "You're not like the others. The way you speak."

I freeze. "Others?"

"Foreigners," he says. "From the Lowlands."

I exhale and give him one more, "Aye," before he nods and shuts the door behind him.

I sink onto the bed and peel my wet clothes off. My stomach growls, but I barely register the hunger pangs. My brain is still scrambling.

The fire crackles in the hearth. The smell of peat and something herbal fills the room. I put on the dry clothes Duncan left. They're scratchy but warm.

This is not a dream.

The way the floor feels under my feet. The flicker of candlelight. The stiffness of wool on my skin. It's all too real.

I stand and walk to the window, peering out. The moon casts long shadows across the courtyard. There are no power lines. No hum of traffic. Just horses, hay, stone, and guards.

And the castle.

This castle. The same one I walked through earlier today. But everything is different now. It isn't an event center, museum, or tourist site.

I'm in the past.

This can't just be some drunken misunderstanding. I'm *here*, and I don't know how I got here—or how to get back.

My thoughts race. I need a story. A believable one. Something that won't get me tossed out or executed or whatever they did to suspicious men with American accents in 16th-century Scotland.

I could say I'm from the Lowlands. That I was attacked on the road and robbed, lost my horse, my companions….

Maybe I'm a nobleman? I was certainly dressed like one when Cait rescued me. Maybe that is why she's being so kind.

But even I know enough history to realize that nobility is dangerous to fake. If only Fiona were here….

Fiona had just told me about the MacRae family right before she slipped off the bridge into the river. And now I'm here with Laird and Lady MacRae, but where is she? Where is Fiona? I hope she's safe, wherever she is.

I rub my eyes. My mind keeps returning to Cait. The way she

pulled me from the water. The physical strength and determination that must have taken. The way she held her ground like someone born to lead.

She saved me. That alone should make me trust her. But I don't know her. And I can't afford to tell her the truth about where I'm from.

Not yet.

I lie back, staring at the ceiling. My heart won't slow down. My body's exhausted, but my thoughts are charged.

This is the sixteenth century. Somehow, impossibly, I've crossed time.

I need to survive long enough to understand how—and if—I can ever get back.

CHAPTER 4

The days after I pulled Rory from the river are a blur of motion, unspoken doubt and wary glances. He walks with the grace of a nobleman, and while Father doesn't say it aloud, I see the caution in his eyes.

Still, Rory's manners win Laird MacRae over. He bows with just the right tilt of the head, speaks with quiet courtesy, and never oversteps his place. He tells us he was on his way to a wedding at a kirk in the Highlands when thieves set upon him in the woods. They stole his horse, his coin, and left him for dead. One of them struck him so hard across the head, he barely remembered stumbling to the bridge before falling into the river. That's where I found him, but cunningly, Rory leaves out how I saved him, telling my father it was a guard who came upon him.

When Rory shares his tale, my father only grunts in reply. But he doesn't press further, and in this household, silence often means acceptance.

Father agrees to let Rory stay for a while. "Just until you find your way again," he says, eyes focused. "But mind you, I'll not have trouble in my halls."

"I understand," Rory replies. "You have my gratitude and my word."

Rory speaks as though he's learned our words from a book, not a cradle. His speech is too drawn out, and sometimes his tongue slips, as if he tries too hard to sound like one of us but cannot quite catch the manner.

But when he moves, when he lifts a bow or spins a blade, there's nothing uncertain about him. He moves effortlessly, like the weapons know him. It's in those moments I forget he's a stranger. It's in those moments I wonder just how much he's hiding.

Rory bests Duncan in archery. My brother scoffs, waves it off, and blames the wind, but there's no mistaking the precision of Rory's aim. He splits an arrow straight down the middle, and Duncan's jaw tightens so hard I think he might crack a tooth.

Then comes swordplay. Duncan's been training since he could walk, and yet Rory disarms him in three moves, not with brute strength but a magnificent technique that spins the blade right out of his hand.

They spar again, and again Rory proves the better, calm and steady, never boastful. His performance is unlike any I have seen before. He holds himself low, knees bent like a cat ready to spring.

Afterward, when they lay down their weapons, Rory shows Duncan a manner of fighting he calls *martial arts*. A strange name none of us have ever heard before.

"What country did you say you were from?" I ask him that evening, eyes narrowed as he sharpens Duncan's dulled blade.

"The Lowlands," he says quickly. "But my tutor was from further off. France. And before that, he'd trained in… the Orient."

It's an odd answer, but there's a sparkle of mischief in his eyes like he knows exactly how odd it sounds.

I begin to watch him more closely.

He eats with a fork when no one else does. He flinches when the church bell rings. Sometimes I catch him staring at the castle walls like he's trying to puzzle them out. Once, he asked me if there were secret passages. When I laughed and said there might be, he looked so delighted you'd think I'd handed him gold.

I can't decide what to make of him. He's clever and kind, aye, but there's a depth to him. An anchor, as if he's bearing some secret deep within, keeping it from the rest of us, and yet I don't feel threatened by him in the least.

The sun blazes high when Father sends us down to the glen to see to the shepherds and their herds. The three of us, Duncan, Rory, and I, walk with easy steps, counting the sheep, asking the shepherds if they need rest or a meal, the wind stirring the tall grass all around us. It should be a quiet task, but then the silence breaks with a sudden clang of steel.

We hear shouts, deep, guttural and angry. The clash of swords. Duncan swears under his breath. I grip the hem of my skirt in a fist, ready to run.

Rory's eyes snap in the direction of the noise, his whole body tensing like a deer sensing a hunter's bowstring.

"This way," Duncan hisses, grabbing my wrist.

We scramble behind a large boulder at the edge of the field. After a few terrifying moments, I muster the courage to peer out across the meadow. We stand just far enough to see all that unfolds, yet remain hidden from sight.

Highlanders, but judging from their banner colors, not our own. A dozen men on one side, nearly twenty on the other. The smaller force is faltering, fighting with desperate, vicious fury.

One of our shepherd lads comes over the hill, clearly shaken as he realizes he's been caught in the middle of a battle. He runs toward the timber, crying out for his mother, reaching the trees just before the massacre.

Blood spatters on the grass. One man falls, clutching his side. Another swings an axe so wide it catches two at once. The screams make my stomach twist.

I've heard of such battles, grudges between families, land disputes, and honor debts. But I've never seen it. Not this close. Not in our pasture.

"Should we help?" I whisper, my voice nearly gone.

"We can't," Duncan mutters. "We're outnumbered and out-armed. We'd only die."

Rory says nothing. His jaw is clenched, eyes narrow, hawklike. Something about his reaction tells me he's seen violence like this before.

Eventually, the fighting shifts, moving down toward the stream. The sounds grow fainter.

Duncan pulls me back by the shoulder. "Come on," he says. "Let's go before they spot us."

We run, ducking through the trees, taking the long way home, until the castle walls rise in the distance.

Tonight, the hall is quieter than usual.

Father speaks in low tones with a visiting messenger. I catch a few words. "Border tension… MacLeans… warning…. Meggie, the cook, says someone saw a man dragged through the village half-dead, left as a message."

I feel the tremor in the stone beneath our feet. War is on the horizon.

Rory lingers near the hearth, his face shadowed. I sit beside him, drawn to the silence between us.

"You've seen such things before. Pain, torment, death," I say, though it falls from my mouth more wondering than certain.

He exhales slowly. "Yes," he admits. "More than I'd like."

I nod, unsure what to say.

But then he looks at me with gentler eyes. "I hope you never see anything like that again," he says.

Later, in the stillness of night, I lie awake beneath my quilt. I can't stop thinking of him. Rory, with his unshakable calm. The way he speaks, as though our tongue is borrowed, and yet he wins every challenge Duncan throws at him. Moreover, he carries no pride in the victory. He's not one of us. He's not even like the Lowlanders I've known. There's something otherworldly about him.

And how does he know things from the East? He spoke of the Orient and showed Duncan a way of fighting none of us had ever seen, swift and strange, with hands and feet moving like water and fire both. He called it *martial arts*, words that taste peculiar in my mouth. How would a Lowland noble learn such things? Unless he isn't truly what he claims.

I would be wise to keep my wits about me. Words of war stir, clans drawing blades over old wrongs and fresh insults. The air reeks of unrest, like the moments before a storm breaks.

And Rory... Rory is no common traveler. He bears no banner, claims no kin I know, and yet he moves with the ease of a man trained for danger. There's more to him, I can feel it in my bones. He's not what he seems, and whatever truth and knowledge he carries may matter more than I know.

CHAPTER 5

Rory

Dawn slips in slow and foggy, creeping through the window of my bed chamber. The faint chill presses against my skin, but I pull the woolen blanket tighter and listen to the stirring of the castle waking around me. The sounds of horses in the courtyard, the low murmur of servants, and the distant clang of the blacksmith's hammer remind me where I am. A time long before mine, and a place that demands careful footing.

Today will be another day of work. Not with sword or bow, but with ledgers and plans, with understanding the land, its people, and their needs.

Downstairs I find Cait moving through the great hall, brisk and sure. She carries a small leather-bound ledger and a quill, her expression serious, as she consults with a steward. When she sees me, her expression softens, and she raises a brow. "You're up early."

"I try to make the most of the hours," I reply. "Time is not mine to waste."

She smiles, "My father says your ideas help."

I nod, feeling the tug of pride and hesitation mixed in equal measure. "There's much I can do to make business more efficient."

When I spoke with Laird MacRae about the estate's ledgers. He'd asked, almost dismissively, if I knew my numbers. I told him I'd studied trade and market patterns where I came from, carefully avoiding the *when,* and that I had a knack for making coins stretch farther than most thought possible. His brow had lifted, skeptical, but when I pointed out three errors in the estate's grain records and suggested a more efficient rotation for the fields, his skepticism gave way to interest.

Cait leads me to the steward's quarters, where a pile of ledgers waits on a rough wooden table. "Father wants the accounts reviewed. The rents, the wages, the harvest estimates. After hearing about your business practices, he trusts you to help straighten things out."

I take the quill she offers and settle beside her. The task is tedious but familiar. Simple numbers, records, balance sheets, tools of order in a world of chaos. I catch myself slipping into old habits, jotting notes and calculations.

I glance up to see Cait watching me, eyes thoughtful. "You handle these with the skill of a man who's done this all his life."

I shrug. "It's knowledge I brought with me from… home…."

She says nothing more, but her gaze lingers longer than before.

Outside, the sound of hooves signals Duncan's approach. He steps inside, nodding at me, an easy, brotherly greeting. "Any trouble?"

I shake my head. "Just learning the ways of your land."

Duncan's grin is bright. "You're a quick learner, Rory."

Later, as the day stretches on, we turn to matters of protection. Rumors of rising tension between clans swirl like smoke. I speak cautiously of ways to better arm the men, to train them in formations and techniques that could save lives. Duncan and Cait listen intently.

When Duncan leaves for a meeting with Laird MacRae, Cait and I take to working the horses, a chore she insists I learn well.

I catch myself stealing glances at her. Her red curls, the light in her blue eyes when she laughs. Every time I look at her, there's a conflict between my head and my heart. A pull between desire and duty. Between the here and now, and the future I must return to.

One afternoon, as we ride the ridge overlooking the valley, Cait's voice breaks the silence. "You seem like a man of many secrets, Rory. You speak little of your past."

I hesitate, then decide to share a sliver of truth. "I come from far away. A place you would not believe."

Her eyes narrow in curiosity, but she nods, respecting my boundaries.

We ride back to the castle in silence, the sun dipping low and painting the sky neon orange. I feel a pang of guilt for holding back, especially when she looks at me like she's trying to crack a code. She deserves honesty, but how could I possibly tell her the truth? That I come from a time centuries beyond her own? Cait wouldn't believe me. No one would, and I would be banished from the castle. Then where would I go?

That evening after dinner, word comes from Laird McRae: a great hunt is to be held. Lairds from the surrounding lands and clans will gather, a display of strength and alliance. I am to join Laird MacRae, Duncan, and the other men, to witness and learn.

THE MORNING OF THE HUNT BREAKS CLEAR, THE SKY A SHARP BLUE without a trace of fog, an uncommon mercy in this part of the world, where mist usually clings to the hills. The courtyard buzzes with preparation. Horses are groomed and bridles polished. Spears gleam and arrows are fletched fresh.

As I adjust my kilt, Duncan claps me on the shoulder. "You're one of us now, Rory. Ready for the hunt?"

"Aye," I say, not knowing what to expect.

We set out, a company riding in a loose line through the heather. In this era, a hunt like this is a dance of power, a show of might and respect.

I watch Laird MacRae take the lead, his voice commanding as men on horses scatter through the woods.

The wind cuts sharp against my face as we ride, hooves thundering across the uneven earth. Duncan is ahead of me, crouched low over his horse's neck, urging the beast faster. I keep close, eyes locked on the flash of russet in the distance. Red deer are sleek and swift, bounding through the undergrowth like smoke.

I've never hunted like this, never galloped full-tilt through wild country with a bow and centuries of tradition on my back, and yet it feels natural.

We crest a ridge, and I catch a clearer view of the animal. Antlers like branches, muscles straining to jump out of harm's way. It's beautiful, especially in flight.

Duncan raises his bow and lets an arrow fly. It misses by mere inches. The deer veers again, crashing through a shallow stream.

Over the next bend, Laird MacRae appears like a ghost, his horse in a steady run beneath him. The deer bursts into the open, hooves skimming over the unbalanced terrain and in one fluid motion, Laird McRae rises in his stirrups and aims his spear. It sails through the air with precision, striking the red buck clean through the chest.

The beast stumbles, staggers, and collapses with a final shudder, its antlers digging into the earth.

Laird MacRae dismounts, and after the animal becomes still, he lays a hand on the deer's flank and whispers something I can't hear. In that moment, I realize this was never just about the hunt, or the animal. It was about legacy, and proving he still has the presence and strength to lead.

Next, I see Cait, standing beside a man with a broad, toothy grin and eyes that gleam fiercely. He stands close, too close, to Cait. His posture is possessive, like a wolf who's already marked his territory. There's a flicker of something primal in the way his gaze sweeps over her, a silent claim that turns my stomach. Cait doesn't shrink from him, but she doesn't meet my eyes either. And that, more than the hunt, makes my pulse drum in my ears.

"Lachlan Drummond." Duncan's voice breaks my thoughts. "Her betrothed."

The word betrothed lands harder than I expect. Lachlan Drummond. Of course she'd be promised to someone like him. He fits in this world in a way I never could, as the chieftain of his clan. I steady my expression, forcing it to stay neutral, and silently pray Duncan hasn't noticed the way that single word has rattled me.

That night, as the fire blazes and men share tales of glory and battle, I sit apart, caught between worlds. I have won their trust, earned a place among them, yet the future calls out to me, louder than ever.

Cait's laughter floats across the hall, but I force myself to look away, wondering why I am so drawn to her.

Every moment I spend here pulls me further from the only thing that matters: finding a way back home.

CHAPTER 6

Cᴀɪᴛ

My mother's voice is sharp with purpose this morning. She stands at the foot of my bed, arms crossed, gaze expectant.

"We'll need to decide on the fabric," she says before I've even swung my feet to the floor. "And you'll need a proper seamstress. One who won't gossip if we choose something finer than the usual."

I sit up slowly, blinking away sleep. "Fabric for what?"

"For your wedding gown and veil, of course," she says, as if I should've expected her to be in my bedchamber at dawn for discussions on linen and lace.

I nod silently. If I speak, I'm certain I'll ask why this talk must come before I'm fully awake, when we haven't even settled on the wedding date.

Lachlan is everything a nobleman ought to be. Strong, well-bred, proud, but I feel nothing when I look at him. No warmth in my cheeks. No tingles when he looks at me.

Alas, he's a good match. A political match. My father approved the union, sealing it with a firm nod and a handshake over mead.

Now, the only feeling in my heart is disappointment that my life, my future, can be traded away so easily, simply because I am a woman.

But I don't tell my mother that.

"Mother," I say gently. "You should design my gown."

She looks hurt. "I thought you might want to be part of it," she says softly. "The dress, the flowers… it's your wedding."

I choose today's work clothes hastily and step behind the curtain to dress quickly.

"When I imagined this time in your life, I thought we'd plan it together. I thought we'd laugh," my mother says from the other side of the room.

"You've always had better taste than I have," I say as I step around the curtain, walk over to her, and kiss her cheek.

A shadow passes through her expression, and for a moment, she looks older.

Guilt pricks sharp beneath my ribs. "It's not that I don't care," I explain. "I just… I don't know what I want yet."

She tries to smile, but it doesn't reach her eyes. "That's why mothers are here, Cait. To help their daughters figure out which direction to go."

I wrap my arms around her. "Then I trust you. Every party you've ever planned has been fancy and elegant."

Before she can say more, I slip out of the room, pulling my shawl around my shoulders. I need air. I need space. I need to ride my horse, Lua.

I step into the stables, the familiar scent of hay and horses wrapping around me. Rory is already here, sleeves rolled up, brushing down Eira, our oldest mare.

I exhale, relieved. Around him, I don't feel like the daughter of a laird or the future bride of a man I barely know. He never expects me to be graceful or agreeable or anything other than exactly who I am.

I'm just Cait.

Rory hums as he works. The melody is soft, beautiful and haunting, yet unfamiliar. I pause, picking up a pail of oats balanced on my hip, and tilt my head toward him.

"What's that you're humming?" I ask, stepping closer.

He glances up, as if startled to have been caught in a private moment. "Oh. Just an old song," he says, a bit too casually.

"Well, I gathered that much," I tease. "But what do they call it?"

His eyes dart around the stable, then back to me. For a breath, he seems to weigh his answer. "It's called *The Long and Winding Road,*" he says finally.

"That sounds… lonely," I nearly whisper, stepping closer to him. "Is it a sad song?"

Rory shrugs, and there's a hint of melancholy behind his forced smile. "A little, maybe. It's about a path that doesn't lead where you expect. Or maybe it does, just not the way you thought it would."

I consider asking him more, but when his gaze drops to the ground, I know better than to push.

"It's beautiful," I say instead. "Who composed it?"

"McCartney," his response.

I'm shocked. "Not Henry McCartney of Edinburgh?"

"No, this McCartney is Paul. From Liverpool."

"Paul McCartney from Liverpool? I've not heard of him."

"He's not very well known yet," Rory says, his expression shifting, a spark of amusement lighting his features.

His good humor seems to return. I'm not entirely sure why. Maybe he just loves talking about music.

We continue our work, preparing the horses for the day, the tune slipping back into the air between us.

I approach Lua, my towering bay stallion with his glossy black roan coat. His thick mane ripples in dark waves. I saddle and mount easily, and with a gentle nudge of my heels, Lua trots out to the meadow.

We thunder across the field, hooves drumming a wild rhythm on the soft earth. The wind whips through my hair, tossing away the heaviness of my betrothal and the future. For this moment, riding full speed with Lua, I taste freedom, raw, fierce, pure and exciting.

After running across the open land, I ease my horse to a gentle trot. The thudding of his hooves softens as we enter a shaded woodland path, the canopy above dappling the sunlight in shifting patterns. The fresh scent of pine and juniper berries surrounds me, but my thoughts drift back to Rory.

He is exceptionally careful when he speaks of his past, I've noticed. There's always a hedged word, a glance toward something I can't see. He says he's from the Lowlands, but I've met men from there before. None of them spoke like he does. Rory has ideas I don't understand. He references things I can't quite grasp. But I won't pry. Not yet. Perhaps there's a part of me that enjoys the mystery.

Duncan is often at our father's side now, sitting in on meetings and learning what it means to run the estate. Rory and I are left to the tenants, herds, the ledgers, and the horses. Often, I find myself looking for him when he's not near, which makes guilt prickle beneath my skin.

Lachlan is to be my husband. Lachlan, whose family controls the trade routes and passages to the north. Marrying him would make us stronger, more secure. It's what's expected of me, and I never wanted to disappoint my father, not when he's placed such trust in me.

As Lua and I move slowly along the shaded path, I realize how different I feel around Rory. He speaks softly but seems to see everything. He's taught me things I've never even considered. When I'm with Rory, I feel... wilder. More alive.

With him, I am seen, not as a prize to be won or a bargaining chip, but as a person. A friend. He listens, respects me, treats me like an equal, and that makes my heart ache with a quiet longing. I wish that all men held women in the same regard.

Lua's hooves drum a steady rhythm against the earth as I guide him back toward the stables. Once we round a bend near the old pasture wall, I spot Rory crouched by the fence, a hammer in hand. He pauses, wiping sweat from his brow, and looks up as we approach.

"Need a hand?" I call out, already slowing Lua. He smiles, and I swing down from the saddle without waiting for an answer.

I hold the post and he hammers. A long moment passes before he says anything. "Do you love him?"

It's abrupt, and it's not a question people ask here. Love and marriage don't often live in the same house.

"Lachlan? I barely know him," I say carefully. "And something about him puts me on edge. But marrying him would be good for the clans... and that's what matters, isn't it?"

Rory doesn't reply. He only nods once, eyes on his work.

"Rory," I say softly, "why do you stay here with us instead of traveling on? Surely there's more road ahead for you."

He pauses, looking up with a half-smile. "It wouldn't be wise to travel alone these days. The clans are at war on the borders. Danger lurks on every path."

I nod, knowing the truth behind his words.

"And," he continues, "I owe the MacRaes for their kindness and shelter. It's only right I repay them however I can."

I raise an eyebrow, waiting for him to elaborate.

"Well," he adds with a grin, "even if it's by mending fences... or helping their remarkable daughter get better with her bow."

I feel a flush rise to my cheeks. "Remarkable?" I ask timidly.

He shrugs, returning to the fence. "You are more than that. You're brave, clever, and the best company I've found here."

I can't help but smile at the compliment.

We help each other with a few more tasks. Later, when we part ways for the day, I glance back and find him watching me, his expression unreadable.

That night, my mother returns to my bedroom, laying out bolts of wool and linen, her fingers brushing over each fabric with reverence.

"Imagine the guests," she says. "All of them watching you walk toward Lachlan in something truly splendid. A bride as beautiful as you, a sight they'll never forget."

I nod, but all I can think of is Rory, and the strange things he says that make me laugh long after he's gone. The way he looks at the world as if it's both familiar and foreign all at once.

I'm supposed to marry for politics, for family, for peace.

But my heart... my heart is wandering.

And it's not wandering toward Lachlan.

CHAPTER 7

Rory

I stand beside Cait. She holds the bow with a quiet determination that never ceases to surprise me. Her fingers find the arrow's nock with steady precision, drawing the string back without hesitation. The release sends the shaft zipping toward the target with a satisfying thud.

She's not the sheltered noblewoman her mother might think she is. Cait is sharp, quick, and fiercely loyal, trading her own joy and freedom for political alliance. Cait puts her people, her family, her land, and the people who depend on her, above herself. She would've made a great SEAL.

I watch her and feel a pull I can't explain, a desire to protect her, to stand beside her. But there's the other side of me, the part that knows this time is dangerous and foreign. That knows I don't belong here and that the path home might be the only way to survive.

Cait turns toward me, and I see that she's noticed the way I watch her. For a moment, everything disappears. I step closer, my fingers brushing lightly against hers as she hands me a fresh arrow.

The spark between us is sudden, electric. Something unspoken passes between us. Is it a promise, a question, a longing? I lean in, tempted to find out, to reach out and touch her cheek, to feel the warmth of her skin beneath my hand.

But then the sound breaks through the stillness: hooves pounding hard on the earth.

I turn to see Lachlan.

His horse charges into the clearing, dust swirling in his wake. He dismounts with ease, and his eyes sweep the scene sharply, landing on Cait and me with unmistakable suspicion.

Cait stiffens beside me, stepping back. I do the same, tension coiling tight in my chest. Lachlan strides forward, all the ease replaced with a cold formality.

"Cait," he says, "I see you've found company."

I'm reminded again how little I belong here, how much she belongs to this world, and worse, to him.

Cait doesn't answer right away. Her facial expression remains poised, but I see in her eyes, what looks like irritation, maybe even embarrassment. She's not a woman who likes to be caught off guard.

"Just practicing," she says evenly. "Rory has a good eye for form."

Lachlan's gaze lingers on me for a moment too long. He nods once, but there's no warmth in it. "Aye, he seems to have an eye for a great many things."

The words are casual, but the undertone slices clean and sharp. Cait shifts beside me, but I keep my expression neutral, forcing my hands to remain loose at my sides.

I know his type. Egotistical, territorial, and used to getting what he wants. And I've already seen enough to know he considers Cait part of his territory.

"Well," Lachlan turns to me, "you'll want to keep practicing, then. You'll need more than luck if things go poorly."

I've been deployed to war zones, infiltrated hostile compounds, and stood face-to-face with men who wanted me dead. And yet, resisting the urge to knock this guy out is harder to swallow.

A voice cuts through the quiet.

"Oi! There you are!"

I turn to see Duncan walking toward me, a bow slung across his back. "I'm gathering lads to train with the longbow, tenants and their sons. Thought you might lend a hand."

"Sure," I say, falling into step beside him. "Happy to help."

We bid Lachlan and Cait farewell and head for the trail, the woods thinning as we lead our horses through low brush and broken stone walls. Duncan's quiet for a bit, chewing a strip of dried meat as we ride. Then he speaks.

"My father's sending messages to our allies. The Campbells, Gibbons, Boyds, and a few others up farther north. Says it's only a matter of time before skirmishes turn to something more."

I nod, already expecting this. "He's right. Once fighting starts, it spreads fast. Nobody wants to look weak."

"Aye," Duncan mutters. "And none of us want to be caught with our breeches down when it comes."

He pauses, then shoots me a glance. "You've seen war, haven't you?"

I hesitate. "Yeah. I've seen it."

He nods slowly. "Figured. You fight like no warrior I've ever met. Like you see what is coming in every direction all at once."

We ride in silence for a bit, and I appreciate Duncan not being more interested in my past. I let my thoughts drift. The land here is raw and untamed, like something out of a dream or a memory. And the people are proud and strong, bound to this earth with blood. If war comes, they'll fight. And if they do, they'll need every edge they can get.

Maybe that's why I'm here.

I know tactics, formations, how to move men through trees without a sound. I know pressure points, weak spots in armor, how to improvise a trap or turn a blade at the last second. It's in my muscle and bone, the product of years of training, hard-earned scars, and harder-earned instincts.

I could help them survive.

But even as the thought takes hold, something inside me resists. No matter how much I'm needed here, no matter how much I'm starting to care, I wasn't meant to live and die in this time. I didn't come here by choice, and I don't know if I can stay by choice, either.

Still... for now, I can teach. And maybe, for now, that's enough.

The boys gather in a ragged circle. Most of them are lanky, all elbows and knees, clutching their bows with the eager clumsiness of youth. A few older lads, barely men, stand among them, trying to look confident but glancing sideways at Duncan and me for instruction.

Duncan starts them off with stance and posture, his voice steady but patient. I can see the pride in his eyes. These boys are kin, neighbors, and the future defenders of his clan. Maybe mine too, if I stay.

"Feet shoulder width apart. Anchor the string at your cheek," I say, demonstrating slowly. "Don't just pull. Aim. Breathe. Think of the arrow like it's part of you."

A few of them try, but their arrows veer off wildly. One thunks harmlessly into the dirt ten feet away.

I chuckle, walking over to correct a boy's grip. "Not terrible, but keep your elbow higher. Like this."

I lift my bow and loose an arrow. It sails clean and true, striking the target dead center. A hush falls. Then a few gasps.

One of the older boys murmurs, "Did you see that?"

The boys see me differently now. Less like a stranger, more like someone to follow. I show them again, slower this time, and soon they're lining up to mimic my form, correcting one another, even competing.

It's strange how natural this feels. Not just the teaching, but being part of something that happened so long ago, yet it's unfolding right in front of me. This isn't a reenactment or a history book. It's real. It's now. And somehow, I'm in the middle of it.

Duncan claps a boy on the back. "Better, lad."

On the ride back, the sun begins to sink low, burning gold on the hills. Duncan and I ride side by side.

He casts me a glance. "You're staying, then?"

Duncan is nothing if not frank. I hesitate. "For now," I nod.

But part of me aches to go home, to find a way back to my time.

It's not just the hot showers, large supreme pizzas and late-night talk shows that I miss. I miss my friends, my family, my career….

And yet, deep down, a part of me sees the wild beauty of this place. Duncan's unspoken brotherhood. The mix of storm and grace in Cait.

Strange how a place you never meant to go can feel like the place you were meant for.

CHAPTER 8

CAIT

The moment Rory and Duncan disappear down the trail, Lachlan steps closer.

"You shouldn't spend so much time with him," he says, his voice low, controlled. "The Lowlander."

I cross my arms, forcing my expression to remain neutral. "His name is Rory."

"Aye. Rory." Lachlan says it like a curse. "He's not one of us."

"And yet he follows my brother to teach lads to shoot longbows, and he mends my father's fences."

I turn my gaze toward the woods where Rory vanished moments ago, trying not to show how much I miss his presence already.

Rory genuinely recognizes me, not just the dutiful daughter, not just the bride-to-be, but he sees all of me. And that terrifies me almost as much as it thrills me.

"You're to be my wife, Cait," Lachlan reminds me, his hand reaching for mine.

I allow him to hold my hand, but only for a moment, feeling the expectations of the castle behind me. The eyes of the clan.

I need space. I can't breathe.

"I'm going for a ride," I say, turning on my heel.

"Eh? Now?" Lachlan asks with disdain.

"Aye."

I whistle, and Lua comes trotting from the pasture, his dark bay coat shining ebony in the sunlight.

Lachlan watches me mount with a scowl, but he doesn't stop me.

"Ye take care now, Lachlan," I say with a wave.

I urge Lua forward, pressing my knees into his sides, and he darts across the meadow. My braid waves behind me like a flag, and for the first time since Lachlan approached, I can breathe.

The land blurs around me as I let Lua run as fast as he can, his hooves pounding the earth. I cling to the saddle, my thighs burning from the effort, but I don't slow down. If I could outrun the future, I would.

I don't want this life.

I don't want a cold wedding to a man who speaks to me like I owe myself to him. I don't want to be confined to a castle while the world burns outside. I want to *fight*. I want to *choose*. I want to *lead*.

I want...

Rory.

The thought cuts through me like a knife. I close my eyes and see his face, so clear, so full of deep understanding I can't quite explain. When I feel the brush of his fingers on mine, my whole body tingles and then melts.

I know, with sudden certainty, that the life I've been handed isn't the one I was meant to live.

Lua starts to veer toward the woods and I pull him back, aiming instead for the ridge that overlooks the valley. I let him gallop, reckless and free.

Then I hear them.

Hooves. Behind me.

At first, I think it's Duncan or Rory. Perhaps it's Lachlan, having chased me down to continue the conversation I never wanted to start. But something's wrong. These aren't the hoofbeats of a lone rider catching up.

There are too many. Too much speed.

A ripple of unease slides down my spine. Lua snorts, sensing it too. His ears twitch and he tosses his head.

Then I glance over my shoulder. And my blood runs cold. Six riders. Rough, and wild looking. Not MacRaes. Not friendly.

They whoop and shout, kicking their horses faster, trying to surround me. One of them rides dangerously close, grinning with broken teeth. Another flanks me from the right. My heart slams against my ribs.

They're driving me toward the cliff.

Lua's breath is ragged, his ears pinned back. He stands on his hind legs, kicking and landing hard. Trying not to slide off, I tug hard on the saddle horn.

Now we are boxed in with the edge of the bluff looming closer behind us. One wrong step and we'll both plummet.

I can't outrun them, and it's too steep here to go over the edge. That leaves only one option. They've caught us.

One of the men dismounts, grabbing me by the arm. I shriek as he yanks me from the saddle, which causes Lua to kick again. The man tosses me to the ground hard. My back hits the earth with a sickening jolt. Air flees my chest. For a moment, I can't move. Can't breathe. Then the pain rushes in.

Lua bolts. I'm relieved he got away before they hurt him.

The man who pulled me from my horse grins as he looms over me. His face is twisted, lips chapped, eyes wild with whatever twisted joy he finds in this. "Well now," he says. "Look what we've found."

Another dismounts, kicking away my bow. "You'll fetch a fine price," he growls. "Bet yer da will pay handsomely for ye."

They circle me like wolves, stinking of sweat and brandy. My hands curl into fists, my body tense for a fight I know I won't win. I will *not* beg. I will *not* scream.

I'd rather die on this ridge than let them take me.

Then—

A whistle.

Sharp. Familiar. Duncan.

One of the men turns, just in time for an arrow to sprout from his neck.

He drops to the ground.

The others shout, reaching for weapons, but another arrow flies from the trees, slamming into a second man's chest. He topples backward, eyes bulging in shock.

"Duncan," I whisper.

From the shadows of the trees, he rides out, bow drawn. Rory follows behind, eyes burning with fury.

"Get away from her," Rory growls, and for the first time, I hear the full weight of his voice. It's lethal. Cold steel.

A raider lunges toward me, but Rory drops him mid-step with an arrow to the temple.

The fight is brutal, but brief. When it ends, only Rory, Duncan, and I remain standing.

I stagger to my feet, shaking. Blood spatters my dress, and my legs feel like water.

Rory dismounts and is at my side in two long strides. "Cait." His hands are on my shoulders, steadying me. "Are you hurt?"

I shake my head, but the tears come anyway.

"I thought… I thought I was going to die."

"You're all right." He presses his forehead against mine, voice rough. "I'm here now, Cait. You're safe."

Behind him, Duncan sinks to a knee, clutching his arm.

"Duncan!" I move to help him, but he waves me off.

"'Tis nothing," he mutters. "Just a scratch."

Rory checks Duncan's wound with practiced ease. "We need to get back. You're bleeding more than you think."

Duncan nods, grimacing.

We ride back and after Rory helps me mount his horse in front of him, his hand never leaves mine. The adrenaline fades, and what's left is bone-deep exhaustion.

But underneath it, something else has settled.

Resolve.

I refuse to pretend any longer.

I won't marry a man I don't love. I was nearly taken today. Nearly killed. War is coming, whether I wear Lachlan's ring or not. We all feel it. Pretending otherwise won't save us.

Whatever happens next, whatever it costs, I choose my own life. My own path.

CHAPTER 9

The ride back to the castle is slow, the air tense. Duncan's arm is wrapped tightly with a crude bandage made from the hem of my dress, and he groans every time he shifts on his horse. I keep sneaking glances at him, worried he's hurt worse than he admits. Rory rides silently behind me.

We approach the gate where guards give us curious looks but say nothing. Duncan dismounts and strides inside, his pace brisk despite the pain. He probably needs a sip or two of whiskey to knock out the sting before the surgeon looks at his wound.

Rory and I stay behind, tending to the horses. Lua had returned to the stable, just as I knew he would. His flanks heavy with sweat from the run, I loosen the reins, running my hand over his warm neck.

Rory's gaze catches mine, the fire in his eyes smoldering.

"You're safe now," he says, voice low.

I nod, but the tremble in my chest won't settle.

We step into the stable and close the doors behind us. Rory's hand brushes mine briefly. Then, before I can think, he steps closer. The world narrows until it's only us. His lips are soft against mine, and the kiss pulls the breath from me. It's powerful and tender all at once. When we part, his eyes search mine.

My breath catches, a sudden fever blooming deep inside me. He cups my face in his hands, and I lean into him, feeling the beat of his heart against my chest.

Rory kisses me again, his lips moving against mine with a softness I never expected. It's as though he's trying to tell me without words that he'll always be here for me.

When we finally part, the silence feels too loud. I blink up at him, cheeks flushed, pulse pounding. "Rory...." My voice is barely a whisper, caught somewhere between disbelief and a desperate wish.

He smiles, that slow, almost shy curl of his lips. "I've wanted to do that for a long time."

The honesty in his words wraps around me like a cloak, warming the cold edges of my doubt. I want to believe it. But the knot in my stomach tightens. This won't be simple. It may not even be safe.

I glance around the stable, suddenly aware of the shadows. "We shouldn't," I say, trying to steady my voice. "Not yet. There's too much at risk ... too many eyes."

Rory's hands fall from my face to grip my shoulders gently. "Then we'll wait. But I'm not letting go of this." His gaze is serious now, full of promise. "Not of you."

For a heartbeat, I almost believe him. I almost believe that maybe, just maybe, I could choose a different path. One where my heart isn't chained to a contract or a cold alliance.

But then the weight of the world settles back on my shoulders, heavy and relentless. The clan. My father's expectations. Lachlan's claim. The danger lurking beyond the castle walls. It all threatens to tear this moment apart.

I step back reluctantly, rubbing the back of my neck. "I want this to be real, Rory. I want it more than anything. But I don't know how to make it work."

He steps closer, lowering his voice. "We'll find a way. Together."

The promise hangs between us, fragile yet hopeful and strong. I want to believe him. I *need* to believe him.

Lua's soft whinny pulls me back to reality. Night is falling.

I cast one last look at Rory, my heart a storm of faith and fear. "Thank you," I whisper.

He nods, a small smile lingering. "For what?"

"For rescuing me and reminding me there's more to life than duty"

He reaches out, brushing a stray lock of hair from my face. "You rescued me first."

As we walk toward home, the taste of his kiss still fresh on my lips, I realize this night has changed everything.

Nothing will ever be the same again.

A FEW DAYS LATER, THE SOFT KNOCK AT MY CHAMBER DOOR PULLS ME from the quiet thoughts swirling in my mind. "Cait, may I come in?" my mother's voice floats through.

I set my hairbrush aside and rise from the bed, feeling my coarse curls fall free from my fingers. "Of course, Mother."

She steps inside, her usual regal composure softened by something gentler. "I wanted to speak with you before dinner."

I nod, clutching the edge of the bed to steady myself. "What is the matter?"

Mother crosses the room slowly, folding her hands. "I have invited Lachlan to dine with us tomorrow night." Her eyes meet mine.

I swallow, her words settling over me like a heavy cloak. "Tomorrow?"

"Yes." She smiles faintly. "It's important, Cait. As a lady of this house, you must learn to show unity with your future husband."

I bite my lip, trying to mask the turmoil inside. "Mother, I… I don't know if I'm ready for that."

Her gaze softens but her tone remains firm. "You don't have much choice in the matter. This alliance is crucial for our clan's survival."

I look away, heart aching. Has she noticed how my eyes stray to Rory instead? How my feelings for Lachlan have always been of disapproval and even fear? I want to speak, to tell her that my heart isn't in this match, but the words catch in my throat.

Mother moves closer, placing a gentle hand on my shoulder. "I understand this is difficult, Cait. But you must put duty before desire."

Her words settle over me like a stone. Duty. Desire. Two forces pulling me apart.

"I'll prepare," I whisper, more to myself than her.

The dining hall is ablaze with torchlight, the heavy wooden table polished to a shine. As I enter, I feel a thousand expectations like chains of steel on my feet.

Duncan, whose wound is healing nicely, is seated on Father's right. Mother is seated on Father's left.

Lachlan is already seated, his gaze sharp as he watches me approach. Rory sits a few places away, his posture relaxed but his eyes fixed on me with an intensity that makes my skin tingle.

The meal begins with forced pleasantries. Lachlan's words are clipped, his smiles brittle. Rory's presence is a constant reminder of everything I'm denying myself. I steal glances at him, remembering our kiss.

The tension coils tighter until it becomes unbearable. Suddenly, a wave of panic crashes over me. Memories of the attack, the menacing riders, the cliff's edge.

My vision blurs. The room tilts. I push my chair back, my voice catching in a sob.

"I can't—"

The tears come unbidden, hot and unstoppable. I stand, trembling, and flee through the doorway before anyone can stop me.

I run to the stable. Lua whinnies softly as I mount, sensing my turmoil. I urge him forward, racing toward the far edge of my father's lands. The wind tears through my hair, but this time, it doesn't clear the storm in my mind.

At the base of the mountain, I tie Lua to a sturdy tree limb, his dark eyes calm and understanding. Just beyond is the narrow entrance to the cave I've known since childhood, my secret refuge where the world feels less heavy.

I slip inside, the cool stone walls wrapping around me like a shield. The faint scent of earth and moss fills the air. I sink to the familiar floor, the silence like a healing balm. My thoughts swirl.

War is coming. I can feel it deep in my bones, the rumble of clans who hunger for my father's land.

I will be forced to marry Lachlan, a man whose name tastes like poison on my tongue.

And yet, I am drawn to Rory. His kindness, his fire. They stir something wild and forbidden in me.

How can I choose between duty and desire, between safety and freedom?

I clench my fists. I will not marry Lachlan.

The cave darkens as dusk falls outside, but within me, a fierce resolve kindles.

I will find a way out of this betrothal.

CHAPTER 10

Cait

The wine cellar is damp and cool, with the scent of oak casks. I press my hand to the stone wall, letting the chill bite into my palm as Rory crouches beside the lowest shelf, brushing cobwebs aside to reach a bottle of my father's best whiskey.

"Found it," he declares, holding the glass bottle up triumphantly.

"Careful," I say, swatting a strand of hair out of my eyes. "If you break that, Father will skin us both."

Rory grins, all charm and mischief, that crooked smile of his sparking something warm in my chest despite the cold. "A proper Highland execution. At least we'd go out in style."

I roll my eyes but can't help smiling. Ever since our first kiss in the stable, a kiss that left me stunned and breathless, we've found every excuse to be alone.

A walk through the orchard; an evening lesson with the longbow; whispered conversations in shadowed corners. Every glance between us carries a charge now. Every touch lingers longer than it should.

Perhaps someday… more.

A sudden crash above us yanks me back to the present.

We don't move.

Overhead comes a shouting match. Another crash. Glass breaking. A woman's scream.

I whisper. "That was my mother."

We both dart to the shadows of the far wall, crouching low behind the barrels as the muffled noise above sharpens. We hear men yelling, and heavy thuds like people being thrown against walls.

I cover my mouth with my hand, choking down a scream. Rory pulls me against his chest, both arms around me, and I press my face into him to keep from making a sound.

Boots thump above. A crash. More screams. I'm sure one of them is my brother Duncan. It sounds as though they are dragging him out the door.

Rory leans close, his lips at my ear. "We can't stay."

"They'll find us," I whisper.

He nods. "If they have passed through all the guards and made it into the castle, we are clearly outnumbered. We have to run. Now."

We move like ghosts, silent and swift. I lead him to the side door, the one that opens behind the kitchen garden. We slip out into the dark.

My home. My family. I want to yell. I want to fight.

But there are bodies in the path. Two of the estate guards lie face down near the dovecote, blood pooling beneath their tunics. Then I see Meggie, our cook, sprawled beside the bread ovens, her apron dark with blood. Rory pulls me away as I stumble.

We run.

The night is barely moonlit, but Rory moves like he's been training for this. We run fast and low. He keeps me behind him, shielding me with his body when we cross open ground, motioning for silence with quick, precise hand gestures I instinctively obey.

When we reach the tree line, he kneels. "They went this way," he says under his breath. I blink, stunned.

He points to a patch of trampled grass, the faint drag of a boot heel. "Eight men. Three being dragged. One bleeding."

"Duncan?" I cry.

"Try to step where I step," he replies, leading me off the main path.

We slip deeper into the trees, the castle shrinking behind us. Rory halts so suddenly I nearly crash into him. He crouches, pulling me down beside him.

"Stay low," he breathes, eyes narrowed ahead.

I follow his gaze, and there they are. My parents. My brother. Bound and surrounded by riders in unfamiliar tartans. My mother stumbles, and one of the men jerks her upright. My father, blood on his temple, surges forward but is shoved back. Duncan's face is swollen, but he's alive. They're all alive.

A sob rises in my throat, but Rory clamps a hand gently over my mouth, shaking his head.

The men lead my family into the trees, toward the north road. Rory watches, calculating. "They're not killing them," he whispers. "They're taking hostages."

I want to run after them, to scream, but Rory's grip on my arm is firm. "If we follow now, they'll hear us, and take us too. We need more people, and weapons. That's how we get them back."

I nod again, my chest burning with fear, but there's hope now too. *They're alive.* And Rory knows what to do.

We stay hidden in the bracken, silent as stone, while the rival clan disappears into the trees. Watching them drag my family away, helpless to stop it, nearly tears me apart, but I keep silent so the enemy doesn't hear us and capture us too.

Once we're certain the enemy is out of sight, we move again. The path is rugged, but I know these woods. We need to find my mother's kin, ally clans who will rise with us. We need help, and fast.

Hours pass before we stop beneath a ridge where the wind howls low and bitter.

"Rest," Rory says, guiding me down behind a stand of rock and thorn bush.

I nod, collapsing beside him, trembling.

He shrugs out of his cloak and wraps it around my shoulders before pulling me close. I don't resist. The warmth of him seeps into me, and the shivers begin to fade.

"You were brave back there," he murmurs.

I shake my head. "I couldn't do anything. I saw them take my family, Rory. And where have they gone?"

His voice is firm. "Your family is made of courageous survivors."

I want to believe him. I cling to his strength because mine feels shattered.

"Why? Why did they take them?" I whisper.

"For leverage. For information. Whatever they came for, they didn't get it. That means your family still matters to them. That means they'll keep them alive."

I nod slowly. "You sound certain."

"I've seen this before," he says quietly. "Raids. Escapes. We'll protect each other, Cait. And your brother will protect your mother and father."

"Don't leave me," I say before I can stop myself.

"I won't."

He brushes my hair back and kisses my forehead.

WE TRAVEL BY NIGHT AND REST BY DAY, HIDDEN IN CAVES. THE Highlands are unforgiving, but Rory adjusts quickly, never complaining, always scanning for threats.

One morning, after a breakfast of salmon and wild herbs, I ask Rory to tell me a story.

He tells me the strangest tale I've ever heard, of a man named *Santa Claus*. A plump, bearded fellow dressed in red who lives in a land of snow and flies through the skies in a sleigh pulled by reindeer. Reindeer! One of them, he claims, had a glowing red nose and was mocked for it, shunned even, until one foggy night, that same reindeer became the hero.

I stare at him the whole time, certain he is either teasing me, or his mind has gone *craicte*. Flying animals? A man who breaks into homes to leave gifts?

But the way Rory grins as he speaks, all warmth and mischief, makes me laugh despite myself.

"That's the most nonsense I've ever heard, Rory Graham," I say, after he finishes his fable.

"It's a classic where I come from," he says, stroking my cheek.

"I don't understand half of it, but I liked the way you told it. You helped me forget, just for a heartbeat, and the ache in my chest didn't vanish, but it eased."

We lie down side by side, and I pretend to sleep long after he does, staring up at the cavern ceiling, wondering what kind of fate has tied our lives together.

THREE DAYS INTO OUR JOURNEY, WE REACH THE BORDERLANDS OF Lennox territory.

It's nearly dawn when we spot the riders, a patrol of five, crossing the valley below the ridge we are perched on.

"That's Ewan's crest. Two broadswords in saltire behind a swan."

"Friend?"

"Family," I say. "Mother's kin."

We step out of the trees, hands raised, and the riders draw up short.

"Cait?" one of them calls. "Lady Caitriona?"

"Ewan?" I cry, running forward.

My cousin swings down from his horse and catches me in a bear hug. "Sweet Saint Andrew, we thought you were dead."

"I nearly was." I pull back, shaking my head. "They took Father. Mother. Duncan. I don't know if anyone else escaped."

Ewan looks grim. "Come. We'll take you to the croft. My wife and children will love to see you." He nods toward Rory. "And him?"

"My friend," I say. "He saved my life."

Ewan's expression softens. "Then he's a friend of mine!"

We walk the last couple miles to the Lennox croft, nestled among green hills and curling mist.

"Maisy has been my closest friend since we were bairns running through the heather together," I tell Rory. "Now she's married to my cousin Ewan."

The Lennox house is always full. Children everywhere, laughter and chaos mingling with the smell of fresh bread and stew.

Seeing Maisy here, busy at the hearth, her long, golden hair in loose waves, reminds me of a time before all this darkness settled over us.

She doesn't see me at first, but when she does, "Cait?" she says, blinking, then drying her hands on her apron. "What on earth?"

I step forward, unsure how to explain why I'm there without melting into sobs, but she rushes to me and throws her arms around my shoulders before I can say a word.

"You should've sent word. Is everything all right?"

I can't answer. Not yet. I just shake my head and whisper, "It's good to see you."

She pulls back slightly, searching my face, but says nothing more. Instead, she pulls me into the warmth of the kitchen, putting me to work beside her like old times.

Maisy moves effortlessly between pots and pans, her cheeks flushed from the fire's warmth. She calls out instructions to her many little ones, who scurry about the room, their faces alight with excitement and hunger. Rory chops root vegetables while I knead dough for the second loaf of bread.

The table groans under the weight of food by the time we're done, and the clan gathers around with that comforting sense of belonging I've missed so badly.

Ewan claps me on the shoulder, his steady gaze reassuring. "We'll find them, Cait. Don't worry."

Maisy reaches out, her hand grasping mine. "You're not alone in this. We're with you. All of us."

The candlelight flickers across their strong, determined faces. Despite fear gnawing at my heart, I feel hope bloom, here among those who love me. We will search the hills and caves. We will fight.

We will find my family.

CHAPTER 11

I wake to the smell of breakfast cooking. Cait's still curled beside me on the straw-stuffed mattress, her breath soft against my chest. For a few precious seconds, I let myself believe we are safe. That we are together in my apartment back home in the future, it's a lazy Saturday, and we don't have to get up yet.

A rooster crows outside, breaking the spell. Children shriek with laughter. The whole house hums with movement.

Cait stirs. Her eyes open. "Good morrow to ye. Have you been watching me sleep for long?" she asks with a sleepy smile.

I chuckle. "I just woke up too, I'll have you know."

Downstairs, someone clangs a pot and another trill of giggles erupts.

Cait grins. "It's always like this here. I don't know how Maisy has the energy for all of them."

The long breakfast table is crowded. The air smells of porridge, fried herring, bannocks crisp from the griddle, and sweet stewed apples with honey.

The kitchen is loud. Mugs clink, spoons scrape, and the smaller Lennox children chatter and bicker over who gets the last slice of bannock. Smoke curls from the hearth, and the scent of fried herring and oats clings to everything.

Ewan leans forward, elbows on the table. "We ride as soon as we've had our fill."

I nod once. "We'll need numbers. Quiet riders, fast ones. Anyone loyal to the MacRaes."

"They'll come," Cait says, sounding certain.

"My men and I will ride with you. We'll split at the glen." He looks at Cait. "Do you know where to go from there?"

Cait nods, affirmative.

Maisy looks at her husband with worried eyes. "You'll be careful?"

He reaches over and touches her hand. "Always."

"Keep the children close today, Maisy." Cait adds. "Keep things normal, but keep them safe."

Maisy nods, already thinking ahead. "We should have eyes on the road. If any strangers pass by, we'll know."

"Good idea," I say. "We ride light. No noise."

Ewan's already on his feet, rounding up his gear. "We'll need to move fast before word spreads."

Cait stands beside me, buckling her cloak.

I look her in the eyes. "We'll bring them home," I say quietly.

Ewan clasps my arm. "Aye. We will."

THE HORSES MOVE FAST UNDER US, EWAN'S BEST PAIR, SURE-FOOTED, long-legged, and smart enough to pick their own way across the uneven ground. The morning sun glints off the dewy hills, and our breath fogs in the cold as we ride.

Cait and I go the opposite direction from Ewan and his men at the glen, and head for Gibbons territory.

By midday, the land changes. The ridge lines are sharper, with narrower paths.

"The Gibbons borderlands are rockier, and a rougher ride." Cait slows her horse at the crest of a rise. She lifts her chin, scanning the low valley below.

"There," she says, pointing.

I spot them too. Four riders break from a grove near the tree line, moving toward us fast. They don't look hostile, but their speed says they're suspicious of outsiders. Cait raises one hand and holds it steady.

When the men reach us, they form a loose half-circle, hands near weapons, eyes sharp. They wear rough plaids and bear the look of men used to hard ground and harder winters. Their leader, a man with a gray-streaked beard and a jagged scar down his cheek, eyes Cait for a long moment. Then recognition breaks across his face.

"Lady Caitriona?"

She nods, her voice strong. "Aye. And I come with news. Laird and Lady MacRae and my brother Duncan have been taken by rival clans acting without honor. They attacked them in our home. Rory and I just barely got away."

The scarred man dismounts slowly, as if still taking in the sight of her. "Your mother is our kin. We don't forget kin."

Cait sits tall in her saddle. "We've never broken faith with you. But we cannot hold the line alone now. I ask for aid. Not only to find my family, but to stand against those who'd shatter the alliances our clans have kept for generations."

One of the others speaks up. "Your father stood for us at the last council meeting, when MacAulay tried to press our borders. Said he'd bring his army with him if they showed up here. Word got around and they never showed. Your father is an honorable laird. We will stand with the MacRaes."

The leader nods once. "Aye. War's been in the air, but we thought it was still weeks off. Seems we were wrong."

He turns to me, giving me a good once-over. "And who's this?"

"Rory," Cait says quickly. "He's with me. He saved my life. You'll not find a steadier man in a fight."

That earns me a few raised eyebrows, but no one argues. The leader looks back to Cait.

"You've our spears, Lady Caitriona. We'll ride. You say where, we'll follow."

Relief flashes in her eyes, but she only nods once. "We return to Lennox land by nightfall. There's a gathering starting."

"We'll be there," the man says, and mounts again. "Gibbons don't break their word."

THE LENNOX FAMILY'S LAND IS PACKED. MEN FROM THE LENNOX, Gibbons, Boyd, and Campbell clans stand in a rough semicircle, weapons in hand, eyes on me. These men know how to fight, but if we're going to save the MacRaes, we'll need more than muscle.

Cait steps forward, her voice calm but clear as it cuts through the quiet murmurs of the gathered men. "This is my friend, Rory Graham," she says, glancing at me with steady eyes. "He may not be of our clans, but he is as loyal to the MacRae clan as they come. He's seen battle. He knows war. He can teach us some lessons that will save lives. He's seen things none of us have, and he wants to help us be ready. I trust him, and I ask you to do the same. Let him teach you what he knows, for the sake of my family, and yours."

"All right," I say, stepping forward. "You already know how to swing a sword. I'm here to show you how not to die."

That gets a few tight smiles.

"First—perimeter security. Wherever you make camp, don't just post one guard. Make it four. Overlapping views. Think like the enemy. If you were going to ambush your camp, where would you hide? Clear those sight lines. No blind spots. Rotate the watch every few hours. No one gets sloppy."

The men seem to be listening, so I continue with more confidence.

"Second—signals. No shouting. No noise. If you see me raise a fist —that means stop moving. Do not move a muscle."

I teach them a few more hand signals that will definitely prove useful over the next few days.

"Train your men to read these without thinking," I advise.

Cait watches from the edge, arms folded, face unreadable. I wonder if she's impressed or just worried. Probably both.

"And third," I say, raising my voice so all can hear, "when you control your breathing, you control your panic. In the fight, your heart'll pound, your hands'll shake. That's normal. Breathe in for three, hold for three, out for three. Try it now."

I look around at the men, adjusting their belts and focusing on breathing.

"I respect and honor the sound of your battle drums," I say, loud enough for all of them to hear. "The banners, the horns—they send a message. They show pride. But this fight we're walking into? It's not about pride. It's about precision. We're not meeting them on a field. We're slipping into their camp and taking back what they stole. That means no noise, no warning. We go in like shadows and come out with Cait's family."

These aren't men too proud to learn. They're warriors who've seen enough to know that an edge is worth having, no matter how strange its origin. When I finish, they don't hesitate. They start discussing the hand signals and practicing right away.

THAT NIGHT, AFTER WE'VE SECURED THE GROUNDS AND MADE ROUNDS with torches, Cait and I sit outside, backs to the outer wall of the Lennox grounds. The moon hangs low, painting everything silver, and the distant hoot of an owl drifts through the trees.

Finally, Cait speaks. "How do you know all of these different ways of doing things? Where are you really from?"

I exhale slowly, rubbing the back of my neck. I've gone over this moment in my head more times than I can count. I always thought I'd keep it to myself, that I'd figure out a way back before I ever had to explain. But I can't lie to her. Not anymore.

"I'm not from the Lowlands," I say quietly. "And I wasn't traveling to a wedding when you found me."

She turns to me, her brow raised. "Then where?"

I glance at her, steady and honest. "I'm from the future. The year 2025. A place called Tennessee, in America."

She doesn't laugh. Doesn't flinch. Just blinks slowly, processing. "America? What is America?"

"It's a huge piece of land across the ocean. I know how it sounds… crazy right? I didn't mean to come here. I fell into… something. A break in time…."

She's silent for a long beat. Then, she softly says, "That's why you speak the way you do. Why you have new songs and stories. Why you move like a man trained for a different kind of war."

I nod, relieved she believes me and that I didn't get slapped for lying to her.

"Everything's different where you're from?" she asks.

"Everything," I whisper. "Except fear, hope, and love. I'm sorry I wasn't entirely forthcoming with you, Cait. I… I just didn't know how to tell you."

She looks at me with warmth and understanding in her eyes. "I know how it feels to have to pretend to be someone you're not, in order to blend in with the people around you."

I lean in and kiss her with the weight of the world flying out of every cell of my body. When she kisses me back, everything else—time, war, the ache of not belonging—fades to nothing. It's just her. Just us, and for the first time since I fell into this world, I don't feel lost. I feel like I've landed exactly where I'm supposed to be.

CHAPTER 12

I wake before the sun, my cheek pressed to Rory's shoulder, the scent of smoke and wool in my nose. The fire's burned low, but his warmth is steady beside me.

He's from another time. Another world.

The thought circles like a hawk above my head, never landing. I don't know what I expected him to say last night. A tale of exile, a secret oath, or even some strange Lowland magic. But *the future?*

I should feel *craicte* for believing him, but I do.

His words keep threading through my thoughts like a song I half-remember: *Everything's different where you're from?*

Except fear, hope, and love....

A soft breath escapes me, and Rory stirs. I close my eyes as his arm tightens around me, just for a moment. We're exhausted. We've been worried for too long, braced for too many days.

"Are you awake?" he murmurs.

"Aye." I tilt my head and meet his eyes. "We should get moving soon. I want to reach the river crossing by midday. If we don't run into trouble, we can reach the woods that surround my family's land by nightfall."

We pack just enough to move together without fuss. We take weapons and supplies for if one of us is injured. Maisy wraps bread and smoked meats in cloth, and fills our flasks, as we saddle the horses.

The camp behind us is already stirring with low voices and clinking steel, warriors preparing for the mission.

Ewan and the other clan leaders are out already, scattered through the highlands in search parties. They'll cover more ground that way. And if my family is still alive—*when* they're found—it'll be by a man who knows the land.

But Rory and I ride toward home because I can't wait anymore. I need to see if somehow my brother and parents escaped and made it back to the castle.

Rory follows my lead without question. We ride through the heather, keeping to the edges of the glens and off the main paths.

It's not until we stop to water the horses at a stream that I finally say what's been pressing against my chest all morning.

"I used to think I knew my place in the world."

Rory crouches beside me at the bank, cupping water into his palm.

"I thought I was just a daughter. A sister. I thought I'd have to marry Lachlan or someone like him. I thought the MacRaes would stay strong, that we'd always have peace. But now everything's unraveling. And then you—" My voice falters. "You came out of the mist like a mystery."

He doesn't smile, just watches me, listening.

"I've never wondered about the shape and shift of time before," I whisper. "But now I can't stop. If you came *through*, can you go back? Do you want to return home?"

"When I first got here, I desperately wanted to return home. I didn't feel like I belonged here and that if I got caught in a misunderstanding, I'd be a dead man. But now, I'm afraid."

"Of war?" I ask, ashamed I brought him into my battle.

He stands in front of me and holds my hands in his.

"Of course not. I'm not afraid of war or living in a more primitive time. I'm afraid of losing you."

I throw my arms around his neck, and we fall into a kiss full of fire and need. I never imagined I could care for a man this deeply. Even in the chaos that swirls around us, he keeps my head on straight, and is the one place I find peace and strength.

We ride on.

As we near the ridge line, I notice the birds. Not the crows or ravens that usually circle high, but smaller birds. They are silent, still, hiding. There are no chipmunks, squirrels, or rabbits in sight either.

I halt, raising my hand.

Rory rides up beside me. "What is it?"

I scan the path ahead. "No birdsong."

He nods slowly. "Could have been a skirmish here."

"Aye. It means something has unsettled them."

I slide off my horse and tie the reins low to the ground, motioning for Rory to do the same. We creep forward on foot, through the brush.

"Looks like there's an old shepherd's path here that winds through this crossing..."

And that's when I see it.

Ashes.

The grass is blackened in a wide arc, and a lean-to once used by traveling shepherds is a collapsed ruin, its stone walls scorched and half-buried in soot.

Rory mutters, "This wasn't an accident."

"No," I say, my throat tight. "This is a message."

The fire's cold now, but not old. The tracks are heavy, boots leading both in and out.

I drop to one knee, pressing my hand to the earth. There's blood. Dried, yes, but enough that it is still sharp to the nose.

Rory's hand finds mine. We crouch there, breathing the smoke-stained air, the wind cold around our shoulders. I let the silence settle, hoping for some whisper from the land, some direction.

"We can't go forward this way," I say finally. "They could have scouts ahead, watching the castle. Maybe even expecting us."

Rory nods. "Then we wait. We watch."

We set up camp under a dense copse of pine, high on a rise where we can watch the valley and the path.

Rory builds a smokeless fire just as he showed the others at Ewan's, using a shallow pit and damp earth. He explained how it would be harder for the enemy to notice a fire built in that manner.

I set snares for rabbits, though I don't hold out much hope. The wind has shifted, and the animals can sense the same storm looming that we do.

As the light fades, Rory sits beside me, our knees together.

"I don't know how long I have here," he says softly. "I don't know how it works, or if I'll wake up one day and vanish."

I stare at the fire. "Then stay close until you do."

He nods, quiet. "I will."

I lie down in the grass, staring up at the night. The stars, our old friends. Steady, even when nothing else is.

Rory lies beside me. His fingers find mine. And for a moment, neither of us speaks.

We didn't make it to the castle today, but we made it here together, and that is enough for tonight.

By dawn the wind has calmed, but there's still a bite in the air that makes me pull my cloak tighter around my shoulders. Rory is crouched beside the fire pit, coaxing life from damp kindling, when a low growl cuts through the hush of morning.

I quickly turn. A large dog, thick coated and alert, stands at the edge of the clearing. A collie, I think, though not one I recognize. Its hackles are raised, its eyes fixed on us, and I reach instinctively for the dagger at my waist.

"Easy," Rory murmurs, rising slowly. "That's not a wild dog."

"No," I agree, heart thudding. "But it's acting strange. Could have the sickness."

The dog barks once, sharp and insistent, then darts a few paces away—only to circle back and bark again. It's not charging. It's trying to lead us.

Rory glances at me. "I've seen this before. Some dogs do this when something's wrong, but I don't think it's rabies."

"Rabies?" I inquire. Sometimes Rory's words are too foreign to ignore.

"The sickness you speak of," he replies.

The dog barks again, certainly trying to get our attention. We follow, warily at first. The collie darts through the brush, turning back often, making sure we're still following. After a short climb, we find the cause.

A little lamb lies on its side, bleating weakly. Its hind leg is caught in a snare, likely meant for rabbits. The crude trap has tightened cruelly, and the animal is bleeding.

"Oh, poor thing," I breathe, dropping beside it. The dog circles, whining now, licking the sheep's nose.

Rory kneels beside me. "Hold its head," he says softly. "I'll cut it free."

I do as he asks, murmuring gentle words as the collie presses close. The blade makes quick work of the snare, and Rory examines the wound. "Not too deep. I think the little guy will be okay."

We're binding the leg with a strip from my underskirt when we hear a whistle from the ridge above.

A lad steps into view, a crook in his hand. He stops cold when he sees us.

Rory stands slowly, hands open in peace. I rise too, trying not to startle him. "We found your collie," I say. "And your lamb."

The shepherd's eyes dart from me to Rory, then to the collie, who barks and runs straight to him.

"Well," the lad says, exhaling. "Didn't expect to find company up here."

"We didn't mean to alarm you," Rory says. "Your dog led us right to it."

The lad huffs, his face relaxing. "She's smarter than me most days. Thank you, truly. The lamb might've died."

He kneels to inspect the sheep, nodding at our bandage. "That'll hold. My herd's just over that ridge. You passing through?"

"Aye," I say cautiously. "Trying to avoid trouble."

He nods like he understands more than we know, cuddling the injured lamb in his arms.

"You take care around here, lad. There's nothing but trouble coming. You might work in pairs or even more, for the time being." Rory's tone is soft and sincere.

The lad nods again, and I see the hint of fear in his eyes.

"Be watchful, lad. Return to safety," I instruct.

We part ways but before we are too far away, Rory turns back once more. "What do you call your dog? What's her name?" he asks.

"We call her Lassie," the lad shouts back.

Rory bursts into laughter, rich and bright, and I don't even ask what amuses him so. Just seeing him like this, lighthearted and care-free, if only for a moment, fills me with a quiet joy I didn't realize I'd been missing.

We return to our horses and begin another day.

Side by side, we search for my family.

CHAPTER 13

The forest closes in tighter the farther we go, and the canopy above us weaves shadows across the trail. We've long since left the main paths behind, Cait's idea. Too many scouts and bandits on the obvious paths, she said. Too many men looking for MacRae blood.

Better beasts than blades.

I ride behind her through the tangled underbrush, ducking low branches. It feels like we've entered another world, one where time moves differently and danger lurks behind every tree.

"We'll camp soon," Cait calls over her shoulder, her voice low. "But keep your eyes open. These woods aren't empty."

"What sort of not-empty are we talking?" I ask, adjusting the sword at my side.

"Boar, bear, lynx."

I glance around warily. "Right. So just everything that can maim or eat us."

"Be watchful, and you'll be fine," she says.

The trees shift again, darker, heavier. A fallen trunk blocks the trail ahead, so we dismount to lead the horses over it. As I land, my boot sinks into a patch of mud so deep, it nearly swallows it whole.

I notice the forest around us has grown quiet.

Too quiet.

Cait pauses. Her hand drifts toward the hilt of her blade, and her eyes scan the trees.

"What is it?" I whisper.

She doesn't answer, just lifts her hand and points to the track in the mud. Hoof prints. Big ones. Sunken deep. Fresh.

She crouches to inspect them. "Boar," she whispers. "Male. Alone."

A low grunt echoes from somewhere in the bushes.

We freeze.

Another grunt—closer this time. A crashing through the underbrush.

"Don't run," Cait says, voice tight. "Back up slow. Get behind the tree. If he charges—"

Then I see it.

A flash of brown muscle and gleaming tusks, barreling like a cannonball. The boar is monstrous—easily the size of a pony, with coarse bristled fur and eyes full of rage. There's no hesitation, no warning. Just fury.

"Rory, MOVE!"

Too late.

The beast slams into me.

The air leaves my lungs in a rush as I'm knocked clean off my feet. I hit the ground hard, pain blazing through my ribs. The boar wheels back, snorting, eyes locked on me. I try to roll away, but it charges again, tusks goring my thigh.

I scream.

The horses gallop away in different directions.

Cait shoots the boar with an arrow, just missing the animal. The beast shrieks and turns on her. She dodges, dagger in hand. Plunging the blade into the beast's shoulder proves not enough.

The boar barrels forward, mad with pain, but Cait is faster. She leaps aside, drawing her sword now, and slashes at its hind leg. The animal stumbles.

I try to sit up, gritting my teeth against the pain in my leg.

The boar lunges again. Cait drives her sword into its neck. Blood sprays. The beast gives one last thrashing bellow, then collapses beside me, twitching, dying.

Cait drops to her knees beside me, yanking a cloth from her satchel and pressing it hard to my thigh.

"You're hurt badly," she says, breathing fast. "Stay awake."

"I wasn't planning to nap," I gasp.

Her hands are already moving—pressing, tying, ripping her underskirt into strips. She works quickly, rinsing my wound and packing it with herbs, tying the cloth tight. I bite down on my sleeve to keep from screaming. My head spins. The forest sways.

"Rory," she says sharply. "Stay awake."

I blink up at her. Her hair's come loose in the fight, strands sticking to her cheek. There's blood everywhere, most of it mine.

"You saved me," I whisper.

The horses return, and Cait builds a fire as daylight fades. I watch her gathering branches, setting traps, tending to the horses. She's everywhere at once.

I lie back against the large, fallen tree, leg throbbing like a drumbeat. I try not to pass out.

When she's done, Cait kneels beside me again, handing me water.

"You're pale," she says. "And you've lost a lot of blood. We'll rest here tonight. Then ride at first light."

I take the water. "I'm sorry I couldn't help set up camp."

"It's no trouble. I just worry about how much blood you lost before we bandaged you up. Here, have some dinner."

She offers me some of the bread and deer jerky Maisy packed. I chew slowly and feel a bit better. My leg throbs and stings.

She lowers herself to the ground next to me. I grip her wrist, firmly. "Cait… that boar would've torn me apart, and you didn't hesitate. You were calm. Brave as hell. You didn't flinch, didn't back down. That kind of courage? That's rare. I've seen men twice your size freeze in the face of less danger." I pause, my eyes locking on hers. "You didn't just save me. You put yourself in front of something deadly, and you put it down. You've got more heart than anyone I've ever met. You saved me. Again."

She shifts closer. "You scared me."

"You didn't even hesitate."

She grows quiet. "I hesitated. Inside. I just didn't have time to act scared."

I watch her for a moment, the firelight soft on her face. "Thank you."

She meets my gaze. "Don't thank me yet. We're not home."

But her fingers find mine again, and for a while, I forget the pain.

We sit by the fire in silence. Tonight, we've built it higher, not to keep men away—there are none out here—but because the wild things tend to fear flame.

MORNING COMES PALE AND COLD. CAIT HELPS ME TO MY FEET, AND though every step sends pain shooting through my leg, I manage to climb onto my horse.

We ride slowly, carefully, taking breaks every few miles. By midday, the forest begins to thin. Sunlight spills through the trees in long golden beams.

We're almost there.

Almost.

Cait looks over at me. "Still alive?"

"For now," I force a smile. "Will you tell Duncan I was gored by a hog the size of a house?"

"I'll tell him *you* saved *me* from it," she laughs.

"Liar."

She laughs louder, and it makes the pain fade, just a little.

As the castle towers rise in the distance, I look at her and know two things:

I've never owed anyone more than I owe her.

And I've never wanted anyone more than I want her.

CHAPTER 14

Cait

High on the ridge overlooking my father's pastures, the wind whips sharp. My braid snaps against my back as I stand beside Rory, favoring his wounded leg. The pink horizon spreads wide and the land is familiar beneath. The rolling moor, thick forest, and farther away, the curves of the loch.

But it's the smoke that steals the breath from my lungs.

A dark pillar, rising angry and fast. There's too much smoke for a cook fire, too windy of a day for any planned brush burn.

Smoke billows black above the tree line, just past the glen where the nearest village lies. Not strangers. Not far-off neighbors. Our village.

"My God," I breathe. "That's near the north bend. The village."

"Where Duncan and I taught the boys to shoot a longbow?" Rory asks, tears brimming his eyes.

"Aye."

We don't wait. Rory grits his teeth and climbs stiffly into the saddle, pain etched deep on his face. I mount and spur hard toward the smoke. Trees blur past.

Please, no. Please let it be a false alarm. A barn, maybe. Not homes. Not people.

But I know better.

We crest the final hill and the forest breaks into a hellscape. Ash swirls like snow. Blackened beams stab from collapsed roofs. The village is gone, reduced to piles of rubble. Charred walls still hiss with heat.

I slide from the saddle and run, heedless of the danger.

"Cait!" Rory calls behind me, but I barely hear him.

Bodies lie where they fell. A few crawl from the wreckage. They are burned, bloodied, coughing through soot. Children scream and cry.

"Lady Cait!" a voice calls. A lad, his face streaked with ash. He limps toward us, dragging a woman who sobs, incoherently trying to plead for mercy.

"What happened?" I ask, grabbing his arm.

"MacIntyres," he gasps. "They came at dawn. Dozens. We tried to fight. Laird MacRae led us but—" his voice breaks. "He told me to run. He said to find Duncan."

My father is alive. Duncan is alive.

"Where is Duncan?" I ask, frantically.

"Find a place to rest, lad. I will be back to help you," Rory instructs.

We move through the wreckage slowly now. My boots crunch over the debris of shattered homes. The stench of burned flesh and hair clings to everything. Beside the well, I see the healer's hut burned to its stones. A body lies face down across the threshold. My stomach churns.

Rory grips my hand suddenly. "Cait. Look."

He nods toward a crumbled stone wall—once an old blacksmith's hut. A figure huddles behind it, cloaked in smoke and shadow. I recognize the torn plaid before I see the face.

"Father!"

I run, falling to my knees beside him.

His chest rises, barely. Blood stains his clothes, pouring from his neck, pooling on the ground beneath him. His sword lies useless at his side, half the blade snapped off. His eyes open, unfocused, but then they find mine.

"Cait... my lass."

"Father, no—stay still. I'll call for the healer—"

"No time." He coughs, blood on his lips. "Listen. Duncan... he escaped. Took your mother with him."

Rory drops beside me, trying to stanch the bleeding, but my father pushes his hand away.

"It's done. My wound... too deep."

"No, don't say that," I whisper, pressing my forehead to his.

His hand lifts weakly, brushing my cheek. "You've always been strong. Fierce like your mother. Now listen to me, Caitriona. You'll lead them. You and Duncan. He must rally the clans. Find Drummond, Lennox, Boyd, Campbell. We need every ally. Reinforcements must come."

"We will," I choke out. "We will. I promise, Father."

His breath is weak. "Tell your brother... he's the MacRae now." He smiles faintly. "You'll do well, my lass. You always do."

And then his body goes still.

I hold him there for a long time, my face buried in his chest. Rory lays a hand on my back and says nothing. There's nothing to say.

The wind shifts. From somewhere in the wreckage, a familiar whistle.

Duncan.

We find him dragging aside charred beams with a handful of others. His face is filthy, his shirt torn and scorched, but he's alive. When he sees us, he stumbles forward.

"You *are* here," he breathes, pulling me into a hug. "The lad said it was you but I—didn't know where you were. I thought—I thought you were gone."

"We were scouting the ridge," I say, still holding onto my dear brother. "We saw the smoke."

He pulls back, eyes wide. "Where's Father?"

I lower my head, and my silence is enough.

Duncan's jaw clenches. His eyes brim with sudden grief, but he doesn't crumble. He nods, once.

"What happened?" Rory asks, wincing as he shifts his weight.

"They took us that night," Duncan says. "Surrounded the house. Overpowered the guards. We fought but—" he breaks off. "They wanted prisoners, not corpses. They tied our hands, led us north. Said they'd ransom us or keep us as leverage."

"Why let you go?"

"They didn't. We escaped last night when they stopped to camp. Father and I freed ourselves of the bindings, helped Mother and we snuck away. They caught up at dawn when we made it to the village. We fought. The whole village fought like hell. That's when they set everything ablaze…."

My throat closes. "Where is Mother?"

Duncan's face twists in pain. "I lost her. I was in the midst of hand to hand combat and she hid. I can't find her now."

We search for Mother. I start with the place I know she'd go first, where the youngest children were hidden during past raids. A small cellar beneath the potter's shop.

The shop is nothing but black ash and half a wall now. But the trapdoor remains.

Rory and Duncan heave aside the charred beams, their hands raw and blackened with soot. Beneath the wreckage, the trapdoor lies half-melted, its iron hinges twisted by heat. The wood groans as we force it open, the scorched edge crumbling under our grip.

Smoke billows out in a slow, choking breath.

I drop to my knees and crawl into the narrow opening, the scorched boards hot beneath my palms. The air inside is thick and unmoving, heavy with ash and silence.

No one caught down here could have lived.

"She's here," I whisper.

Mother lies slumped over two small children, shielding them even in death. Her face is pale, lips blue. No wounds, just soot and stillness.

"She died trying to save them," Duncan says hoarsely.

We carry them out together.

We work through the day and well into the night. Duncan organizes the able-bodied while Rory, limping but determined, helps carry the wounded. I press cloth to burns, pour water into trembling lips, and whisper comfort where I can. There is no time to cry. Not yet.

We load carts with those too weak to walk and guide the others, the bloodied, barefoot, hollow-eyed, along the narrow trail home. My home rises above us like a promise. Its walls have never looked so comforting and strong.

Inside, we turn the great hall into a place of refuge. Blankets cover the stone floor, fires blaze in every hearth, and the kitchens never stop. Bread, broth, clean water. Simple things, but they matter now.

The injured are laid out gently. I keep moving—checking wounds, stoking flames, wrapping shawls around shoulders. Every time I pass Rory, our eyes meet. He consoles me even without words.

Our people have lost everything, but they are not alone. We will hold them close. Feed them, heal them. Keep them safe.

We place our parents side by side in the chapel. Duncan stands tall, his face carved from grief and fury. When he speaks, his voice is low but unwavering.

"My father died defending our land. My mother died shielding our children. We will honor their legacy and we will not let this go unanswered."

The crowd murmurs, some nodding, others weeping openly.

"We rebuild," Duncan says. "We send word to every friendly clan. We do not mourn in silence. We prepare for war. For justice."

I stand between Duncan and Rory. The three of us, side by side.

They struck our hearts.

We'll show them what happens when a MacRae bleeds.

CHAPTER 15

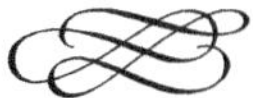

Rory

The great hall is filled with leaders of allied clans, and the tension is sharp enough to cut steel. The crackle of torchlight dances along the stone walls, but there's little warmth here. Men stand in clusters. Warriors with blood still on their boots, elders cloaked in furs, women with red-rimmed eyes and arms crossed tight across their chests. The scent of smoke still clings to everyone, coating the room in sorrow.

Duncan stands near the hearth, his chin high, shoulders squared like he was born to bear the weight suddenly dropped on them. But I see the pain in his eyes. The grief just barely kept at bay. The exhaustion stitched into his frame.

"I did not ask to lead," Duncan says, loud enough to quiet the room. "But I will. I must. My father named me his successor, and I will see his dying wish fulfilled."

A ripple of voices answers him. Some shake their heads. Others whisper to one another. Skepticism stirs.

"He's but a lad," an older man mutters, not quite low enough.

"Aye, and where was he during the last battle?" someone else snaps.

"He was but a bairn during the last battle!" A warrior hollers, causing everyone to laugh.

"No," I say. It comes out firm, and a bit harsher than intended. All eyes swing to me, the stranger. The outsider with the strange speech and stranger ways.

Silence falls.

"You will not find a stronger leader, nor a wiser hand to guide us, than Duncan MacRae. He is, without question, your Laird and rightful chief."

Murmurs stir again, softer this time. Some avert their gaze.

"Who are you to speak for our clan?" a woman asks, not unkindly, but pointed. "You wear no colors. You carry no name we know."

I take a breath. Cait is watching me from the side, her hands clasped in front of her, knuckles white.

"I'm Rory Graham. A traveler. A friend. A man who owes his life to the MacRaes. You're right. I wasn't born here. But I have fought in many battles over many different lands, and I know a good leader when I see one. I know what happens when people turn on each other instead of standing together."

I see that I have their attention now and continue with my point.

"We cannot afford to be divided. Not when our enemies are burning villages and abducting families. Many of you doubt Duncan because of his age. I understand that. You see a young man and wonder if he can carry the weight of a clan. But I want to remind you of another leader. A leader who began with nothing but faith and a stone."

A few heads tilt, curious.

"King David," I say. "He was a shepherd. The youngest of his brothers. Overlooked by everyone—except the God who saw his heart. When his people faced a giant, it wasn't the seasoned warriors who stepped forward. It was David. A lad with a sling and courage no one could measure."

I pace slowly, letting my words settle.

"He became king not through age or lineage alone, but because he led with strength and compassion. He unified a fractured people. He fought for them. And when he failed—and he did—he admitted it. He listened. He changed. That is leadership."

I glance at Duncan, who stands silent but steady beside me.

"Like David, Duncan may be young. But I've seen him bleed for his people. I've seen him stand when others fall. His heart is strong. His cause is just. And if you follow him, you will not only survive—you will endure. You will rise."

Duncan turns toward me, a mixture of surprise and gratitude in his eyes.

"This is no time for an argument," I continue. "It's a time for courage. For grit. For unity. And that means standing behind the man Laird MacRae trusted. That means standing behind Duncan."

A wave of unanimous agreement ripples through the crowd, spreading from face to face. Murmurs of assent swell into firm nods and murmured approvals, the tension easing as doubts give way to trust. Even the most skeptical elders lower their gazes in quiet respect, their hands falling to their sides in reluctant acceptance. In that moment, the hall feels united, bound by a shared hope and the unspoken promise that Duncan MacRae will lead them true.

"We will fight, many clans as one," he says, stepping forward. "We send word to Drummond and Lennox. To Boyd and Campbell. To every soul who has stood with us before. If they won't come for alliance, they'll come for blood. Because the MacIntyres made war on us. And they will not go unchallenged!"

Voices rise now, not in protest but in readiness. Men clasp arms. Women nod solemnly. I feel the shift like thunder beneath the stone.

"We send our fastest riders. Messengers who know the woods and the high roads. We ask for swords, supplies, and sanctuary if it's needed. Not just revenge, but defense. We protect what remains and rebuild what's been taken."

Later, when the last rider has been dispatched and the hall has emptied into shadow, I find Cait in the chapel.

Candles flicker beside two shrouded bodies. Her parents lie still, honored with simple garlands. She kneels, back straight, hands in her lap.

She hears me behind her.

"I keep thinking I'll wake up," she says. "Back on the ridge. Watching the sunrise. Before all of this happened."

"I know the feeling," I whisper. "I used to wake up hoping I'd somehow be back home. Back in my own time."

Her eyes shimmer, no longer dry. "I need you to stay."

"I'm not going anywhere."

"Not just for the clan, or Duncan, or the people. I need you for me." Her voice breaks. "I need you at my side—not as a visitor, not as a guest, but as my partner."

There's no air in my lungs for a moment.

She reaches behind her and lifts something from a velvet wrap. A sword. Her father's. The hilt is engraved with the MacRae crest—a fess between three mullets with a lion at the base.

"I want you to have this," she says. "You stood by us when you didn't have to. You bled for us. Spoke for us. My father saw something in you. I do too."

I take the sword gently. It's heavier than it looks. Weighted with legacy. "This is more than I deserve."

"It's exactly what you deserve."

I stand slowly, unsheathing the blade. It gleams silver in the candlelight. For a second, I see myself as they do—not a castaway from another century, but a warrior. A protector.

When I look back at Cait, I see her as I first saw her. When she was standing in the middle of a rainstorm on the stone bridge, her cloak soaked, her face drawn in curiosity and wariness. That moment changed everything.

"You remember the bridge?" I ask.

She nods. "You looked like a drowned cat."

I laugh for the first time in days.

When I catch my breath, I take Cait's hand. "I wouldn't just stay here for you. I would die for you."

She doesn't speak, just rests her head against my chest. I wrap my arms around her, silently wishing I could take away all her pain.

In this chapel, where death and grief still linger, we make a silent vow. The world we each knew is gone. What remains must be built by hand, by heart, by determination.

THE WIND COMING OFF THE HILLS IS SHARP, AND COLD ENOUGH TO sting. Dusk creeps in, soaking everything in shades of purple. Smoke curls from the torches lining the edge of the clearing. People stand in rows, quiet and unmoving, like they've attended hundreds of funerals before.

Laird and Lady MacRae lie on stone slabs in the center of it all, wrapped in thick plaid cloth. The tartan is bright red even in the fading light. Duncan said it stands for blood and honor.

Cait stands next to Duncan, straight-backed, hands locked in front of her. Both look stoic, strong.

They've just lost their parents, in a single breath, and yet they look like they're ready to lead a clan, because that's what's expected.

The bagpipes begin, low and haunting, and the sound hits me hard —grief like a fist to the ribs. I've never heard anything like it. It isn't just music; it's mourning in its rawest form.

The earth is cold and dark as they lower the coffins into the ground. Cait doesn't cry. Duncan doesn't flinch. They just watch, steady and silent, like this is the last duty they owe their parents.

Whoever did this—whoever stole them from Cait and Duncan— they'll answer for it.

I swear it.

CHAPTER 16

Cait

The scent of peat smoke and porridge clings to the air as I break a hunk of oatcake and dip it into my bowl.

Rory passes me the honey with a smirk. "Here, you'll need this."

He's still not quite used to the food we eat in this era—claims he misses something called *McDonald's breakfast*.

"Are you missing your McDonald's breakfast this morning?" I ask, raising a brow.

"Perhaps," he says, that familiar twinkle in his eye.

Duncan leans in with a shrug. "I don't see the difference. McDonald sounds Scottish to me."

Rory laughs and bumps his knee lightly against mine under the table. I let it stay there longer than I should.

Before I can think of a sharp reply, the door creaks open and a messenger lad steps in.

"I bring word from Drummond. Laird Lachlan Drummond," he announces.

My spoon clatters into my bowl. Rory's smile fades.

I break the seal before Duncan intercepts the message. My fingers are steady, but inside, everything quakes.

Lady Caitriona, rightful betrothed of Clan Drummond—

Word reaches me that you remain at your family's home in these troubled times. Though I was wounded in the raid against my estate, my strength returns, and with it, my resolve. I come now to claim you as my bride, by the oath sworn between your father and myself before his passing. As your rightful husband, I will provide you safety and position worthy of your name. I will retrieve you within the week. Prepare yourself.

—Lachlan Drummond

I let the scroll fall to the table. "Prepare myself," I echo softly. "*Retrieve me?* As if I'm a room to be furnished or a lamb to be dressed for slaughter."

Duncan reaches for the scroll, reads it, and exhales sharply. "I didn't realize the Drummond estate had been attacked. How have we not received word? It was bold of him to send for you so soon after our parent's passing."

"Bold?" I rise to my feet. "He all but declares I belong to him."

"It's the old way," Duncan says. "A betrothal made and blessed, especially by Father, is binding. You know that."

My temper snaps its tether. "I also know Father's not here to speak for himself, and I'll not be wed off like a parcel to strengthen Lachlan's position."

Duncan raises an eyebrow. "You'd rather stay here? And do what? Lachlan will end ties with us and it will start an *even bigger* war! *You* will start a war. Cait, the clans gather for battle. This isn't a game. If Lachlan can offer you safety, and remain an ally...."

"Safety?" I interrupt. "Lachlan's estate was raided. He couldn't even defend his own lands." I stare at my brother. "You'd let him take me, to score favor with the elders, to make them believe you're strong enough to lead. You'd trade me like a pawn?"

Duncan's gaze falters. "That's not fair."

"Isn't it?" I demand. "You are ready to send me away so you don't have to answer to the men who doubt you. You don't think I can hold my own, even after everything I've trained for. You look at me and still see the little girl who followed you around the yard with a wooden sword, begging to be taught. But that girl is gone, Duncan. I trained beside you and the same men who follow you now. I bled in the snow, blistered my palms, learned to fall and rise again. Every scar I carry, I earned with grit and steel. Not as your sister, but as a warrior. You say you want to protect me, to keep me safe. But safety isn't what I want. Not when our people are threatened, not when our home is at stake. I was born of this land, same as you. My fight is here. You were trained to lead. I was trained to endure. And I have. Through grief, through duty, through every lesson no one wanted to teach a girl. But I learned them anyway. I earned my place, Duncan, just as you."

The silence that follows is brittle, like ice about to crack. Duncan doesn't meet my eyes. He gathers the scroll and folds it again, his motions too precise to be anything but a mask for anger.

"Fine," he says curtly. "You'll stay. But when the fighting starts, you listen to me. No recklessness. No proving anything. You stay alive."

"I'll do what's right," I say coldly.

He nods once, turns, and walks out of the hall.

The moment the door shuts, I let out a breath I didn't realize I was holding. Rory stands beside me, unsure whether to speak. I press my fingers to my temples.

"He would've sent me to him," I whisper.

"I hate that he even considered it," Rory says quietly.

By midmorning, the mood in the castle shifts as the thunder of hooves echoes across the hills. I step onto the western courtyard with Rory at my side and we stare in wonder.

Warriors arrive in waves, mounted men with flying banners of allied clans, foot soldiers trailing wagons stacked with supplies, archers and scouts in smaller bands. They fill the fields outside the castle walls like a swelling tide. Some pitch tents, others begin fortifying the outer perimeter. Wooden palisades are driven into the ground for shelter and protection, and the watchtowers are set with watchmen.

Duncan stands below near the outer gate, speaking to a pair of warriors. Even from here, I can see the tension in his shoulders, the weight of command settling over him.

"Have you ever seen so many?" I ask.

"Only once," Rory replies. "And it wasn't for anything this noble."

I look at him. "You believe in this fight?"

"I believe these people are worth fighting for."

For a moment, I imagine what it might be like, riding out with the others, sword in hand. Then I glance toward the southern road, imagining Lachlan, smug and condescending, demanding I leave with him, and a fever rages inside me.

"I won't let him take me," I say aloud.

"He won't," Rory promises. "Not with you, me, and half a thousand warriors standing between him and the gate."

I can't help but smile.

Below, Duncan lifts his hand to the crowd. Cheers rise up, a vow of allegiance echoing through the valley.

"I never wanted this for him," I say. "To bear the burden alone."

"He's not alone," Rory replies. "You're still here."

I glance sideways. "And we have you here, as well. I don't know if I would have the courage to fight without you, Rory. "

"I know you would, but I'm glad you don't have to go through any of this alone either."

The sun climbs high, and with it, the chaos of preparation. Tents spring up like mushrooms after rain showers, and Duncan calls a war council with the clan leaders.

The council chamber smells of ash and damp stone. Torches flicker along the walls, casting long shadows on the faces of the gathered elders, a dozen gray-bearded men and women seated at the long oak table. I can feel their eyes on me as I step between Rory and Duncan, my head high even though my heart pounds against my ribs.

They fall silent when we enter. Duncan's jaw tightens, and Rory gives me the briefest nod before we stop before the council. I don't wait to be spoken to.

"You must already know why we summoned you here," I begin,

voice steady. "You've heard that Lachlan Drummond is riding here to claim me as his bride."

A murmur passes through the room like a ripple across still water. I press on.

"He claims the betrothal was blessed by my father. And perhaps it was, but my father is not here to speak to his wishes. And I—" I lift my chin. "—am not a prize to be claimed by a man too weak to protect his own lands."

"Watch your tongue, girl," growls Elder Boyd, leaning forward. "Drummond is of noble blood. He offers peace and protection."

"I am not asking for peace," I say. "I am offering strength. You want to protect this clan? Then let me fight for it. Let me stand with my brother and the warriors of Clan MacRae."

Another elder snorts. "A noble woman, on the battlefield? It wouldn't be safe."

I hear Duncan shift beside me, but I raise a hand. "You speak of safety while you'd see me handed off like cattle to a man who sees me only as leverage. Where is the safety in that?"

Rory steps forward. "She fights better than most men I've trained beside. She's no liability. She's an asset."

"She is also a symbol," says one of the elder women gently. "The daughter of the late chieftain. If she dies—"

"If I die," I cut in, "then I die as my father would've wanted, fighting for the people I love. Not locked away in Lachlan's hall, bearing children for a man I despise."

Silence.

I glance sideways at Duncan. He takes a deep breath before speaking. "I will be honest. I considered sending her away. I knew it would bring favor, ease doubt about my leadership… but if I claim to lead this clan, I must do it with truth. And the truth is, Cait has trained for this her entire life. And more importantly, it's her life. She should be allowed to choose her own path."

He pauses. "I trust her, and I want her at my side in battle."

Elder Gibbons frowns. "You risk much, Duncan MacRae. If she falls—"

"If she falls," Rory says, "then she'll fall fighting with a sword in her hand, not lying beneath a man she never chose."

Never before have I been seen so clearly, heard so truly.

With an appreciative nod to Rory, I step forward one last time. "This is not just about me. This is about what kind of clan we want to be. One that clings to tired traditions? Or one that honors strength, loyalty, and choice?"

I take a breath. "You want warriors? I am one. I am MacRae, born of this soil. And I will not be exiled under the name of marriage while my home stands on the brink of war."

The room falls into silence once more. The fire crackles. Somewhere outside, a horse whinnies, a reminder that war waits just beyond the walls.

Finally, Ellen MacRae, my father's great aunt, the oldest among all of the elders, nods slowly.

"You've spoken with courage, Caitriona. And courage is not something we can afford to send away."

She looks to the others. "Let the girl fight."

Murmurs of agreement rise. Gibbons and Boyd grumble but do not object.

It's done.

I don't smile. I bow my head, respectfully.

And when we leave the chamber, I feel the weight shift from my shoulders, and squarely onto my sword arm.

Let Lachlan come. Let the battle come.

I will be ready.

CHAPTER 17

Rory

The chill of dawn lingers in the air as I step onto the rough grass of the training field. Around me, the warriors of Clan MacRae and their closest allies begin to gather, stretching heavy limbs and muttering among themselves. I can feel their eyes. All seem curious, some look doubtful, many skeptical. An outsider teaching them to fight? How much can I, a stranger from another time, possibly offer?

I clear my throat and raise my voice over the murmurs. "Today, I'm not teaching you the way your fathers fought. I'm teaching you how to survive."

A few eyebrows lift. Duncan stands at the edge, watching with a steady gaze. Cait is nearby too, quiet, arms crossed. I'm grateful for their support.

I draw a deep breath and begin. "The battlefield is chaos. It's brutal and unpredictable. You don't always face one opponent. Often, you face many. You don't always have your weapon in hand. You might lose it, or be outmatched. You need more than muscle. You need strategy. You need to think beyond what's been taught. You need to predict how your opponent will move, before he has the chance."

I demonstrate a technique I learned in a military survival course.

A quick disarm using leverage, not brute force. Fergus, one of the bigger men, steps forward with a practice sword. He strikes, but I sidestep, catching his wrist and twisting the weapon from his grip. He grunts, surprised, then laughs.

"Again," he says, eager now.

We repeat it slowly. I break down the steps: hand placement, timing, shifting weight. "Control the weapon, control the fight," I tell them. "Not strength, but timing and leverage."

Pairs form around me. Some struggle, but they try, adapting the unfamiliar moves.

Next, I tackle fighting multiple attackers. "When you're surrounded, you move," I say, pacing between them, "Keep your enemies in front of you, and use the land."

I weave between two warriors, dodging a heavy blow and pushing one into the other. "Use your surroundings. Rocks, trees, loose dirt. Anything can be a weapon."

The men try the drills hesitantly, stumbling over uneven ground, but determination is building. I see a spark in their eyes. The thrill of learning new techniques, and the hunger to survive radiating through the crowd.

"Remember," I say, my voice rising over their pounding footsteps, "the fight isn't just skill. It's will. The will to stand when you're bleeding, and the will to keep moving when your legs fail."

Hours pass in relentless practice. I shout corrections, encouragements. Duncan joins in, testing their stamina, pushing them harder.

Cait steps forward at one point, brandishing a staff with surprising strength and precision. She pairs with one of the men, outpacing him with swift strikes.

Midday, a messenger rides up. Duncan reads the letter and his face tightens. He pulls me aside, away from the others.

"I've news," he says grimly, handing me the folded parchment.

Scouts have returned from the south. "Lachlan Drummond has ridden to join our enemies," Duncan says quietly. "He must have received word that Cait will not marry him, and his men will fight against us now."

The words hit me like a blow.

Lachlan. Cait's betrothed. The man she's been promised to since long before she and I ever met, will fight with the enemy. Anger roars through me, fierce and hot. This betrayal is not just a political maneuver. It's personal.

"We need to prepare Cait for this," I say, trying to keep my voice steady.

Duncan places a hand on my shoulder. "Aye. And then we'll need to prepare the men. They'll be ready, thanks to you."

We find Cait among the warriors, practicing their longbows. The wind tugs strands of hair across her cheek, and I think she is the most beautiful woman I've ever seen, whether in my time or hers.

I dread breaking even more bad news to her.

Duncan glances at me, nods once, and clears his throat. "Cait."

She turns her head, calm and alert. "Aye?"

"There's word from the spies. Please step aside for a moment." Duncan's voice is low, and careful.

We move back from the men, knowing they won't take the news well, and it's not time for them to hear it yet.

"It's Lachlan," I say. "He's joined the enemy."

Her eyes flick to mine, then to Duncan.

"He's betrayed the clan," Duncan adds. "The scouts saw him riding with MacIntyre, and their allies from the south. He'll be coming for us."

Cait doesn't flinch. She looks down at the stones beneath her feet, then up at the sky, shielding her eyes from the sun. "I felt it," she says. "In my gut. I knew he would find out I wasn't going to marry him and immediately seek revenge, breaking all ties. It was his bridge to burn… he won't like the outcome."

There's no tremble in her voice. She sheds no tears. Hell, she doesn't even look afraid.

"You suspected?" Duncan asks, surprised.

"I did," she replies. "He was always more interested in my bloodline than in me, but I wouldn't be surprised if he had been working with the enemy all along."

"He may have been courting you to get information from Father. Not trusting him, not marrying him–that was the wisest decision you could've made," Duncan says.

I glance between Cait and Duncan, my pulse racing with more than just anger. "Honestly," I say, "I'm glad Lachlan's on the other side. Makes things simpler. Now I don't have to pretend I don't want him gone. I'll have every right to take him out myself." The words come out harder than I expect, but I don't take them back. I mean every one of them.

BACK ON THE FIELD, DUNCAN CALLS THE WARRIORS TO ORDER AGAIN. "Listen closely. Lachlan Drummond has betrayed us. He rides with the enemy. This war is not just steel against steel—it's a war for our lives, for our homes. For honor."

Shock ripples through the group, followed closely by fierce determination.

"We fight for our clan. For our families. For the future. Use what you've learned. Fight like survivors!" Duncan shouts.

Their war cries rise, fierce and unshakable.

"Gather 'round now," Duncan calls, firm and sure. "Rory's to show ye some fighting tricks that may seem strange at first, but they'll keep ye breathing when blades are flying. So open your ears, and pay heed."

The men circle around me, skeptical but curious, their boots crunching against the packed earth. They're used to swords, shields, brute strength. Not grapples. Not speed. Not using someone's momentum against them.

"Lend me your ears," I say, stepping into the center. "I'm going to show you how to take down someone twice your size without using a weapon. It's not about strength. It's all about leverage. Fergus, help me out once more."

Fergus steps forward again, towering over me like he's eager to prove this won't work.

Perfect. I love challenges.

He lunges. I sidestep, grab his arm, hook my leg around his, and twist. His feet leave the ground and he hits the dirt with a loud grunt. Laughter ripples through the onlookers, but it's not mocking. I've heard it before. It's nervous laughter, and shock.

Fergus gets up, brushing off his tunic. "Again," he says with a grin.

We go through it slowly. The shoulder grip, hip placement, and foot sweep. Then I show them how to break a chokehold, how to use an elbow strike to the ribs, and perhaps most importantly, how to fall without breaking a bone.

"Your opponent won't wait for a clean strike," I say. "This is about survival. Getting free. Staying on your feet."

They mimic the movements awkwardly at first, too stiff, too forceful, but they're learning. The muscle memory is building. Duncan watches from the edge, arms crossed, nodding now and then. Even he's impressed.

"This," I tell them, "isn't sport. It's war. You don't win by being fearless. Even the most fearless of men can falter. You win by being prepared, anticipating the enemy's next move, and walking away alive."

They're breathing harder, moving quicker. Focused. Hungry for every edge they can get.

As the sun sinks low, I stand with Duncan and Cait, watching the men prepare for what's coming. I realize that this battle isn't just about the past or the present. It's about carving a future worth fighting for.

CHAPTER 18

The council chamber is tucked deep inside the keep, but we can still hear the voices of the elders and Duncan echoing down the corridor. Rory and I linger just beyond an archway, shielded by a dark, heavy, hanging tapestry. We shouldn't be here–we weren't invited–but Rory's expression tells me he's listening as intently as I am.

Duncan's voice rings clear above the others. "Lachlan Drummond has thrown in with the MacIntyres. The scouts saw the Drummond clan with their warband."

There's a long pause. Then the voice of an elder, "The man we were meant to ally with through your sister."

My stomach knots. Even now, they speak of me like a bargaining piece.

"She made the right choice," Duncan says firmly. "Cait saw what we did not. If she had married him, the enemy would already have our walls mapped and our numbers known. She may've saved us all."

My throat tightens, but I don't step forward. Not yet.

More murmurs. Then another louder voice, "She's brave, we grant that. But she's still a noble woman. If she's to fight, she does so at the rear. We can't risk the enemy taking or killing her. She's too valuable."

Valuable.

Like gold. Like land.

I dig my nails into my palms. Rory shifts beside me, jaw locked and visibly tense.

Duncan speaks again, "She'll despise it."

"It's for her protection," an answer. "And ours. If she falls, it demoralizes the men. We can't allow that."

I've heard enough.

I step forward, out from behind the tapestry, my voice clear and certain. "You'll not speak for me."

The elders flinch, surprised. Duncan looks shocked. Rory steps beside me, silent, a steady presence at my side.

"You fear I'll fall and shatter the morale of the men?" I demand. "Then let them see me fight and rise again. Let them see I bleed and stand. That is what will strengthen them."

"Cait—" Duncan starts, but I raise my hand.

"I will not hide on the back lines. This is my clan too. If Lachlan's coming for us, let him see me in the front. Let him know he didn't scare the clan MacRae."

A sudden clamor jolts me from my thoughts. Steel scrapes, boots thunder against stone, and the sharp cry of a lookout rings down the corridor. Duncan stiffens beside me, his hand already reaching for his sword. Rory glances toward the window, his hand resting on his sword, as well.

"What *now?*" I mutter, heart pounding.

Without another word, the three of us push through the heavy door of the council chamber and stride out into the courtyard.

The wind slaps my hair into my face as we hurry up the steps toward the outer wall. Soldiers and servants alike are swarming the battlements, all peering out to the distant ridge beyond the fields.

"Up there," one of the watchmen shouts, pointing. "Riders!"

I squint against the midday sun. Dozens—no, hundreds—of mounted warriors crest the hill like a black wave, sunlight flashing on helms and blades. They move fast, too fast. My stomach flips.

"Is it Drummond?" I ask, turning to Duncan. "Has he come early?"

His face is pale beneath his beard, but unreadable. "I don't know," he says tightly. "No scouts warned of this."

Rory is already pulling his belt tighter, his eyes fixed on the ridge. "If it's an attack, they're smart to come from the high ground."

"A watchman calls down from the tower, voice sharp with urgency. 'Hold fast! I see their crest—two broadswords crossed behind a swan.'"

"The Lennox crest," I breathe. "That's Ewan."

Duncan releases a long breath. "Aye. It's Ewan Lennox."

Cheers ripple along the wall as the realization spreads. The tension melts from the soldiers' shoulders.

Ewan and his warriors thunder down the hill, a clan of hardened fighters and fierce loyalty riding to our gates.

The gates are thrown open, and I race down to meet them. Ewan dismounts before I reach him, his face ruddy and wind-chapped but smiling.

"You came," I say, breathless.

He grips my shoulders with rough hands. "I couldn't sit at home while my kin went to war. I've got children, aye—but I want them to have a future. And that means fighting for it."

Emotion swells in my throat. Behind him, the Lennox warriors line up, proud and ready.

I clap Ewan on the back. "You're just in time."

I step forward, heart pounding, eyes scanning the gathered crowd. The air is filled with hope now that Ewan and his men have joined us.

"Men of the clans, hear me!" I roar.

The crowd falls silent, expectant.

I raise my chin, steadying my voice. "Ewan Lennox has come here today, leaving behind his wife and children—the very ones he swore to protect. He has ridden into danger, not because he wants glory, but because he knows what it means to fight for what matters."

Murmurs ripple through the crowd. I press on.

"If Ewan can find that courage, then so can I. I am just Cait—a noblewoman, yes, but also one of you. I carry the blood of this land in my veins, and I carry the spirit of our people in my heart."

I see their eyes shift, measuring me, weighing my words.

"I will not stand behind while my kin face the enemy. I will not sit safe while others bleed for this land. I will fight for my home, my family. I do not ask for permission," I say, my voice ringing clear across the courtyard. "I ask for your trust. Trust that I will fight as fiercely as any man here."

The first cheers break out, swelling into a roar. Hands raise, voices shout, drums beat.

The elders throw up their arms in weary surrender. They see now there's no bending my will.

There's no stopping me.

Duncan steps forward, his voice steady but tinged with concern. "Cait, ye can fight alongside me and Rory. But know this—I'll be watching over ye. I won't let harm come to ye."

I meet my brother's gaze, a fierce light in my eyes. "Duncan, ye need not trouble yourself with that. Keep yourself safe. I can handle whatever comes. I'm no bairn to be sheltered."

I smile, fierce and unyielding. This is only the beginning.

THE ROOM STILL SMELLS LIKE MY MOTHER. HER SHAWL IS FOLDED neatly at the foot of the bed, just as she always left it. I sit in her chair by the hearth, the one she favored when mending or reading, and trace my fingers over the worn armrest.

"I wish you were here," I say softly.

I stand and cross the room to my father's side of the bed. The comb he carved for her still rests on the table. I pick it up and hold it in both hands like it's sacred.

"There's going to be a battle soon, " I whisper. "I'm not as wise as you were, Father. I don't have your grace or your strength, Mother. I feel like a scared little lass and I wish you were both still here. And I— I think I'm in love...."

I close my eyes and picture their faces. I wonder if they'd understand. If they'd forgive me for not marrying Lachlan. If they'd scold me for letting a stranger into our home and into my heart.

"I've tried to be brave, and I will fight." The fire cracks softly in the hearth. I kneel at the edge of the bed like I did as a child when I was frightened by storms.

"I still miss you every day," I say. "There's so much I want to tell you. Duncan is strong, unwavering. I hope you would have been proud of us."

My throat tightens, and I fight back a sob. I press my forehead to the blanket and let the silence gather around me.

"I hope, wherever you are, you can see me. I hope you see I'm doing my best for the clan. For our home. For you both."

I rise slowly, the comb still in my hand. I tuck it into the sash for good fortune, and walk out the door, shoulders squared.

I'm ready to be the warrior I promised my people I would be.

CHAPTER 19

The fire crackles softly in the hearth, casting flickering shadows across the stone walls of my chamber. Rory sits across from me, a mug of whiskey cradled in his hands.

It's not proper for a woman of my standing to have a man in her private chamber, but tonight, with the threat of battle looming over us, I set tradition aside.

We've faced death side by side on the run, and shared cold nights pressed close for warmth. Now my room, with its heavy tapestries and the faint scent of lavender, suddenly feels less like a place for solitude and more like a sanctuary when he's near.

Rory doesn't look at me like some prize to be won or even a prize to be protected. He sees me, all of me. He sees my strength, my doubts, my stubbornness. That's something no man here has done before. I'm not meant to stay in the shadows, bound by rules that feel tighter than a bodice. With Rory, I can breathe.

Tonight is not a matter of breaking rules or giving way to sudden whims. It is a chance to truly see one another, for war is upon the horizon, and our hours together may be few. Rory looks at me as if he sees beneath the surface, past the armor I wear for the world, into the parts I hide even from myself. And I want to know him like that. Beyond the warrior, to the man beneath.

"So," I begin, swirling the warm amber liquid, "tell me about Tennessee."

I look at Rory, waiting, curious. He smiles softly, then begins.

"Tennessee," he says, "is a place far from here, across the great Atlantic Ocean. It's a land where many from Scotland and Ireland—your distant kin—will settle, about two or three hundred years from now. The landscape is... familiar in some ways. Rolling hills, forests thick with trees, and rivers that run wild and clear. Scotland reminds me of home."

He pauses, his eyes thoughtful. "The people there—well, they're proud, just like here. Fierce in their loyalty, but friendly too. They hold tightly to their roots and traditions, just like your clans."

I nod slowly, imagining a place so far away and yet somehow echoing this rugged land I know. "So, it's not so different," I say quietly.

"No," Rory agrees. "It's like a little piece of Scotland transplanted across the sea, carrying its spirit with it."

I sip from the cup in my hands, the firelight dancing across the rim. Rory's voice lingers in the air like smoke, his words about Tennessee still settling in my mind. A land that holds echoes of this one—how strange, and how beautiful.

I glance at him, the shadows softening the sharp lines of his face. "Did your country ever go to battle?" I ask.

He exhales slowly, staring into the flames, as if imagining a far off place. "By the year I came from, 2025, America has endured much bloodshed. One of the bloodiest wars was our American Civil War," he says. "It happened about a hundred and sixty years before my time. A brutal fight between the northern and southern parts of the country."

"What were they fighting for?" I ask, my voice quiet.

He looks over at me, solemn. "The north was fighting for the freedom of other men. They wanted to free the slaves and the southern states wanted to keep owning slaves. Can you imagine such a horrible thing to want to continue on? But it wasn't just that—it was power, pride, and fear all tangled together. Families torn apart. Cities burned...."

"Did your people—your family—fight in it?"

"Some," he says. "My ancestors fought. It was a war that tested what the country believed in, and whether it would stand for freedom, or fall apart."

"And did it stand?" I ask.

He nods slowly. "Yes, but it changed everything."

I nod as he finishes, the weight of his words pressing into the quiet between us. I'm curious—achingly so—about this war that tore his country in two, about the echoes of violence and courage that shaped the world he comes from. But I can feel the heaviness settle in his shoulders, the way his jaw tightens when he speaks of it. He's seen things I can't begin to understand, and I know he has seen battle directly.

"I want to know more," I say gently, "about the war, about your people. And eventually about the battles you fought in first hand, but not tonight. I don't want to weigh us down with sorrow," I murmur, setting my cup aside, feeling the whiskey go to my head.

"So tell me something else. Something lighter. Tell me about the music in your time. Do you always sing ballads? Do you dance around fires? What stirs the hearts of your people, Rory, when there's no war to fight?"

His lips twitch into a smile, soft and sudden. "Music?" he echoes, leaning back slightly. "Now that's a topic I can definitely work with."

Rory chuckles, the sound low and warm, easing the tightness in the room. He takes a slow sip from his cup. "Aye, we've got ballads still, though you'd find them played on electric guitars instead of fiddles. And drums that rattle your bones in ways the old war pipes never could."

I laugh softly, already trying to picture it.

"There's a little bit of everything," he says, voice growing steadier. "Country songs that sound like home, full of heartbreak. Rock that makes you feel like you could take on the world. And blues music for the soul, Cait. It aches the way people do when they've lived a hard life and still find a way to play music."

His gaze finds mine, something quiet and sincere in it. "You'd like some of it, I think. Some of it would remind you of this place. Strong voices, proud words, stories handed down in melody instead of ink."

I smile, drawn to the way he speaks, the way he weaves his strange world into something I can almost touch. "Do your people dance to this music?"

He grins. "Oh, we dance. Sometimes in wild crowds with lights flashing and hearts racing. Sometimes slow, just two people swaying in a kitchen with bare feet."

His eyes are on me now, and my heart stirs like a chord struck gently.

I lean forward, intrigued. "And I have been meaning to ask you, how did you end up here, in Scotland?"

Rory takes a sip of his whiskey, the firelight dancing in his eyes. "I was working on a movie set in 2025, called *Where the River Runs Crimson*. I helped them with the battle scenes."

I refill our cups with whiskey, and settle back, curiosity curling inside me. "A *movie*. What is a movie?"

He takes a slow sip, then sets the mug down, thinking. "A movie, or a film is like... a story told with moving pictures. Like when someone tells tales by acting them out, but instead of just words or live shows, we capture it all. We capture people's faces, their words and actions, on film and then we put it in a box that holds light. Then others watch it later."

I frown, even more puzzled. "Film? A box that holds light?"

He nods, smiling gently. "Aye. Imagine the flickering of a fire, but inside a wooden box, showing faces and places, and sounds too. People gather to watch these stories like a play, but it doesn't happen live. It's been caught and saved."

I swallow, eyes wide. "So, a story caught in a box of light for others to see? That's strange... but clever."

Rory chuckles, raising his glass. "Aye. And sometimes those stories are of battles, love, or honor."

I nod, feeling a buzz of warmth, equal parts whiskey, and something deeper. "And what did you say this *movie* story was about?"

Rory's gaze turns thoughtful. "It was about a man forced to choose between staying home to protect his family or joining a battle that could change the course of history. When Ewan showed up this afternoon, I realized the movie was kind of about him."

I stare at him, stunned. "So you're saying the movie was based on real events? On my cousin's life?"

He nods. "Yes, and no. It was based on Ewan and all the men just like him in your time. And now, here we are, living it."

I set my glass down, my mind racing. "It's strange to think that our lives are stories being told centuries from now."

Rory reaches across the table, taking my hand in his. "But right now, this moment is ours."

I look into his eyes, seeing the depth of emotion there. "Yes, it is. Thank you for sharing your story with me," I say softly. "I hope we have time to learn everything about one another."

He squeezes my hand gently. "Thank you for listening."

Rory's touch and my second cup of whiskey warms me from within, a slow bloom in my chest.

"I've never met anyone like you," he says quietly. "Not in my time. Not in yours."

I stand up, barefoot on cold stone, and take the few steps toward him. My heart pounds in my throat, but I don't stop.

"I've slept beside you beneath trees and stars," I say. "I've trusted you with my life, and now I find myself wanting… more."

He rises to meet me, slow as sunrise, and my hand finds his chest, warm and chiseled beneath the thin linen.

"I want to know you the way you seem to know me," I whisper.

He kisses me like he's been holding back for days, for centuries— passionate and sweet. His hand slides to the small of my back, pulling me closer, and I rise onto my toes to meet him. My fingers graze the hem of his shirt, wanting to feel the warmth of his skin, to know he's real and here and mine, at least for tonight.

Rory's hands settle at my waist, and even though I've imagined it before—his touch, the weight of his gaze, the press of his body against mine—nothing prepares me for the aching sweetness of it.

We move slowly, both of us tentative and a little clumsy in the way that first times often are. He treats me like I'm something to be unwrapped, but I tear his clothes from his muscular body.

I lie back against the bed, and he follows. The weight of his body against mine is comforting. We move together slowly, reverently, like we're building something fragile.

His lips find my neck, and I moan as his hands explore my breasts.

"I've wanted to do this with you for so long," he whispers in my ear as his fingers discover my wetness.

I moan my answer, as his thumb moves over my most sensitive skin. Arching my back and moaning, I look into his eyes and say, "Take me, Rory."

The moment he enters me, everything else falls away—the room, the fire, the world beyond these walls. It's too much and not enough all at once. My breath catches, and I cling to him as a wave crashes through me, raw and overwhelming. I didn't know it could feel like this—like my body already knew him, like it had been waiting. I break apart beneath him, trembling, gasping his name like a prayer, and all I can think is *yes*—yes to this, to him, to us.

Afterward, he gathers me against his chest, his fingers tracing idle shapes along the bare skin of my back. The blankets are tangled around us, and for a moment, I don't have a care in the world. I feel warm, safe, and known.

"I didn't expect this," I whisper into the hollow of his throat. "Any of it. You...."

"I didn't either," he says, brushing his lips against my temple. "But I'm glad we found each other."

We lie there in silence, listening to the wind at the windows. I hear the steady drum of his heartbeat beneath my cheek, and for the first time in a long while, I don't feel like I'm bracing for what's next.

I just feel... love.

Rory

The chill of the Highland morning bites through my cloak as I stand at the edge of MacRae land. Mist clings to the hills and drifts through the valley below, silver and slow-moving like breath exhaled from the earth itself. We have the high ground.

This isn't a drill, training exercise, a staged assault with blanks and simulated fire. It's not even a war zone the way I remember it with night vision goggles, satellite intel, and commands in my ear. No. This is dirt, blood, blades, and screaming horses.

This is what war looked like before humanity learned how to destroy itself from a distance. When men could only kill each other eye to eye.

And I'm afraid.

I don't say it aloud, but I feel it in my gut. Not the familiar fear of dying. This morning, I fear for the people I love. For Cait, Duncan, and the lads who have trusted me. Men who've trained under me, who are marching into the face of death because they would rather die than give over their land and villages to the enemy.

I grip the hilt of Laird MacRae's sword tighter and feel the calluses that have formed from practice, drilling day after day with the MacRae men.

Cait stands a few paces away. She's laced into her leather, her long fire-red braid slung forward over her shoulder. She looks calm, but I know that's just the surface. There's fire underneath. There always is.

I want to tell her to stay behind. I should beg her. But of course I won't. She won't listen anyway, and that's one of the things I love about her.

Cait turns to look at me, and for a moment, everything else fades.

"We come back," I say, quiet but fierce. "You hear me? Stay close. Stay safe."

She nods.

Then the war horns sound.

It starts with a low rumble of hooves, then the clang of steel. Shouts echo across the valley. The enemy comes pouring up the hill, clad in a patchwork of armor, axes glinting, spears raised. They're not an organized army, but they're brutal.

"Hold the line!" Duncan's voice rings out.

He's already mounted, sword drawn, fire in his eyes. We've trained for this. I told them to stay tight, fight smart. Don't let chaos swallow you.

We charge down the slope into them, Highland voices raised in fury.

The crash of bodies is immediate. I parry the first blow that comes at me, pivot, and drive my sword into the man's side. He falls, gasping. No time to hesitate. Another comes, screaming with a curved blade. I duck, step inside his swing, and knock him back with the pommel of my sword. He crumples, and I spin, searching the field.

Cait is gone.

I crane my neck, scanning the mess of bodies and horses. I see no sign of her, and my heart threatens to rip through my chest.

I can't protect her if I can't see her.

Someone slams into my shoulder, and I'm down in the mud. A huge man straddles me, axe raised. I roll and twist back, grabbing the knife in my belt, and burying it in his thigh. He howls, falling off me. I jump up and stab him through the heart.

Blood roars in my ears. All around me, the MacRae men fight like warriors with discipline. They're holding their ground. They're using what I taught them. I see them forming pockets, fighting in pairs, flanking.

And it's working.

Still no sign of Cait.

I don't have the luxury of searching anymore. I grit my teeth and fight, slipping into the rhythm I know too well. Assess, react, move, repeat. My old training kicks in, SEAL instincts flooding back. I move through the field like I own it.

Duncan is on my left, fending off two attackers at once. He's still mounted, but one man leaps, grabbing his reins. Duncan goes down hard, dragged from the saddle.

Without hesitation, I run to his side, reaching him as one of the attackers raises a club. I slam my shoulder into his gut, knocking the weapon aside, and take him down.

Duncan's still wrestling with the second one. I drive my sword through the attacker's back before he can land a blow.

Duncan coughs, rolls to his knees. "You're a bloody miracle, Rory."

"Get up," I pant, grabbing his arm.

Together, we rise, bruised and breathless. Around us, the tide begins to turn. The enemy line is breaking. Some flee. Others drop to their knees.

The MacRae banners are still flying. But Cait…?

"Cait!" I yell. "Cait!"

Nothing.

Duncan turns, face grim. "Last I saw, she was with Ewan's unit on the flank. Come on."

We sprint, dodging bodies, weapons, fallen horses. My boots have no traction in the bloody mud, but I don't stop. The end of the line is littered with corpses. I search each face. None of them are hers.

Duncan and I round a cluster of boulders and run straight into another wave of enemy. Four of them, blades up, blood thirst in their eyes.

Duncan shouts, a battle cry, raising his sword.

The first man lunges with a dagger and I step in instead of back, protecting myself with my shield. My left arm deflects his swing, and my right drives straight into his jaw, blade first. He drops like a sack of grain.

Another comes at my side. I drop low and hook his knee, flipping him hard onto his back. He gasps, the wind knocked out of him, and I don't hesitate—I drive my sword into his throat.

The third man swings wildly. I duck his blade, drop my weapons, and grab his tunic with both hands, slamming him to the ground. He scrambles to get up, staggers, and I pivot behind him. Wrapping my arm around his neck, I twist with everything I've got, snapping his neck.

Duncan sidesteps the fourth attacker, and at the last second he drives his sword up through the man's gut. Blood spurts as the warrior lets out a guttural cry. Duncan yanks the blade free and lets the body drop, his chest heaving.

"What the bloody hell kind of training do you have?" he asks.

The bodies around us blur into smoke and blood red. I can't stop. Cait's still somewhere out there in this madness, and I'll burn through an army to reach her.

Duncan and I descend further into the valley, boots crunching over flattened heather and broken shafts of arrows. Blood spatters the rocks.

"Where is she?" I say louder than I intend, fear consuming me.

"She might've taken a wound and crawled off," Duncan mutters beside me. "Might be hiding somewhere."

The clang of steel fades into scattered cries and the low moans of the wounded. The rhythm of combat—boots pounding, blades clashing, men shouting—slows like a dying drumbeat. I stand in the churned mud, chest heaving, blood drying on my hands, and realize the enemy is retreating. Their banners disappear over the ridge, and what's left of our force begins to regroup, some collapsing where they stand. The worst of it is over. The field is eerily quiet now, and yet my heart pounds louder than ever because Cait's still not here.

"Cait!" I call again, cupping my hands around my mouth. "Cait, where are you?"

We find the remains of the Lennox flank, their battle flag lodged in the earth, fluttering in the breeze. A few of the warriors are here, dazed and bloody. I recognize one of them, Callum, sitting against a rock, clutching his side.

"Did you see Cait?" I ask, crouching beside him.

Callum shakes his head slowly. "She fought like the devil," he rasps. "Killed three men before I lost her in the fog. I—I think she was headed east, toward the creek."

That's all I need.

I rise. Duncan stays with his injured kin. "I'll catch up with you, Rory," he calls after me, but I'm already yards away.

She's strong, I remind myself. She's smart.

"Cait!" My voice cracks.

I rake my hand through my hair and turn in circles, trying to see her face in every shadow, every glint of armor or flash of movement.

Nothing.

Duncan catches up to me, breathing hard. "We'll find her."

I drop to one knee, elbows on my thighs, sword dragging in the dirt beside me. "If she's not dead," I whisper, "then she's in danger."

We both know what that could mean.

Lachlan.

Taken by the Drummond clan as a trophy, a hostage, or worse. My stomach turns, and I press my hand against the earth like it might tell me where she's gone.

"We need dogs," I say flatly. "Trackers. Torches. We search all night if we have to."

Duncan nods grimly. "I'll round up who's still able. We'll start back from the glen."

I watch him run through the darkening brush. Alone now, I walk east another few hundred paces, past a stream where blood thins and runs away with the water. I call her name again.

Only the wind answers.

I drop to the ground and stay there, eyes closed, listening.

If she's still out here, I'll find her.

Or I'll die trying.

CHAPTER 21

Bodies lie scattered across the bloodied hillside, and blood pools in the valley below. The earth is dark red now, soaked in a mess of mud and iron. Some still groan where they've fallen, clutching wounds, teeth clenched in agony. Others are somewhere beyond sound. Dead eyes stare at the sky.

My hands are stained scarlet and my arms ache. I don't even remember how many men I killed. I only know she's still out there—Cait—and I haven't found her yet.

"Rory!"

The shout slices through the smoke.

It's Duncan.

I spin and run.

He's maybe twenty yards off, backed against a half-burnt cart, his sword locked against a huge man with wild hair—an enemy chieftain, judging by the cloak he wears and the way others steer clear. Duncan's blade slips. The chieftain drives his own sword forward.

"No!" I yell, sprinting faster.

Duncan gets stabbed in the thigh before I reach the brawl. He lets out a sound I never want to hear again, a cry of pain, rage, and defiance.

I crash into the enemy chieftain with full force, shoulder first, knocking him away from Duncan. The massive warrior swings at me but I duck, roll, and come up behind him, wrapping my arm around his neck. I twist, slamming him backward. We fall together, and I drive my blade through him before he can recover. His body twitches once, then goes still.

I drop beside Duncan. Blood pours from the wound in his leg. He grunts in pain.

"Can you walk?"

He tries but can't stand up.

I sling his arm over my shoulders and half-drag him toward the nearest wagon, wrestling against the pain in my own side. When we reach it, two MacRae men run over to help. "Get him back to the castle," I say. "Tell the surgeons he needs stitching and something strong for the pain."

They nod and begin loading him gently into the cart.

Before they hoist him up, Duncan grabs my sleeve. His face is pale, jaw clenched. "Find Cait," he says.

"I will," I promise, and I mean it with every broken, bloodied part of me.

The wagon rumbles away over the uneven ground, wheels jostling, Duncan's head lolling back against the wooden side. I watch until it disappears into the haze. Then I turn back toward the battlefield.

Bodies of men I trained with, men I laughed with, ate with, taught how to throw a proper punch lie everywhere. Some are curled around their wounds. Some aren't moving at all.

I call her name again.

"Cait!" My voice rips out of my throat raw, over and over. "Cait!"

No answer. Just the wind, and the groan of someone dying nearby.

I move from body to body, pulling off helmets, and scanning faces. I keep searching, over hills and dips, through shadows and smoke.

In the midst of it all, I find Ewan. He's crumpled beneath a fallen horse, his blade still clutched in one hand, his body still. Far too still. I drop to my knees beside him. "No," I whisper. "No, come on."

His eyes are open, staring straight through me. The tears come fast and hot. I don't even try to stop them.

I press a hand to Ewan's forehead, then close his eyes. He left behind such a beautiful family. He was brave, loyal, too young to be cut down like this.

I sit there for a long moment, barely breathing. The weight of everything presses in on me. Cait is still missing. Duncan is bleeding in a wagon. I've been through war before, but this? This isn't a mission. This is family.

This is the woman I love.

I look up at the sky, still overcast and unforgiving. I've never been a praying man, but I do it anyway.

"Please. Let her be alive." I get back up and start looking again.

A few MacRae warriors spot me coming over the ridge. One of them raises a hand. "Rory! Are ye sound?"

"No," I say. "I need eyes out. Cait is missing. Spread the word around, and search for her. And we could still have enemy fighters hiding in the hills. Search in pairs, and keep to the ridge lines. No one goes alone."

They nod, already moving.

Another warrior steps forward. "You're looking for Lady Cait?"

My throat tightens. "Yes."

"We'll find her, sir. If she's alive, we'll bring her to you. If not…?"

"If not," I say, lowering my eyes to the ground, "bring me her body."

He nods solemnly and walks on.

I keep searching, my feet heavy and head pounding. The adrenaline is starting to drain now, and with it comes the pain. My side's bruised, shoulder's on fire, and I can feel blood trickling down my ribs. But I'll search for as long as it takes.

I comb through the valley, calling her name again and again until my throat is raw. Each time I lift a body to check, I brace myself for her face—expecting the worst, hoping against it. I find familiar armor, and familiar banners, but not her.

The hills are quieter now, but every noise still makes me turn, weapon ready. I climb to the top of a ridge and scan the slope below. Smoke curls lazily from a ruined cart. Another MacRae banner lies tattered in the mud. No sign of her.

Then movement catches my eye—two warriors dragging another injured man toward a wagon. One of them glances up and calls to me.

"Rory! You need anything?"

"Have you seen Cait?" My voice is raspy.

They shake their heads. "No one's seen her since the clash by the stream. Might've been separated."

I nod, though it makes my stomach churn. "Keep your men moving. Watch for stragglers."

"Aye," one of them shouts as they move along.

I force myself down into the next valley. The stream runs red with blood. I remember Cait leading horses here once, laughing as water splashed her boots. I close my eyes for half a second, trying to hold onto that sound. Then I open them and keep going.

I pass a crumpled MacRae soldier lying on his side. One arm is bent at a sickening angle. I check for breath. None.

I move on.

Another young man, barely more than a boy, cries out for his mother. I kneel beside him and press a hand to his shoulder. "You're all right," I lie. "Help's coming."

He's bleeding badly from a gash in his chest, and the way his hands tremble tells me he won't last long if he's left here. I glance toward the distant wagon. It is about two hundred yards away. He won't make it on his own, and I can't carry him and keep looking for Cait.

Still, I can't walk away.

"What's your name?" I ask him.

He blinks up at me through blood and dirt. "Tavish. Tavish Graham," he chokes out.

That knocks something loose in my chest. My family tree is full of men named Tavish Graham. Maybe I will be able to save one of them.

He tries to sit up, but winces and collapses with a groan. "I'm sorry—"

"Don't be," I say, already easing an arm beneath his shoulders. "You're going to be fine."

I hook my other arm under his knees and lift. His blood soaks into my tunic, hot and wet, but I keep my grip tight and start moving.

The slope is steep, the ground slick, and each step sends a jolt through my already aching legs. I grit my teeth and push forward. Tavish is mumbling now, something about his mother's bannocks and the way he used to sneak them off the windowsill before supper. I nod along, letting him talk. Anything to keep him awake.

By the time I reach the wagons, I'm breathing hard, drenched in sweat and blood that isn't mine. Two older warriors rush forward. One of them helps lift Tavish from my arms and lays him gently in the back of the cart.

"He needs stitching. And water. He's lost a lot of blood."

"We'll take care of him," one of them says. "You've done enough."

I step back, swallow hard, and turn to the hills again, hoping the lad makes it out of this alive and wondering if he's my distant kin.

There's still no sign of Cait, but I keep walking. Every footstep feels heavier. My lungs burn. I've trained harder, fought longer, but never with this kind of weight on my chest. Never with the fear that someone I love might be bleeding out under a tree somewhere, alone.

The sun starts to dip low on the horizon, turning the hills gold. And still, no Cait.

If I don't find her by nightfall, I'll search until dawn.

CHAPTER 22

The charge comes fast.

One moment, Rory is beside me, his shoulder brushing mine, his voice low and steady in my ear: *"Stay close. Stay safe."* And the next, the world explodes into chaos. Horns blare. Arrows scream overhead. A stampede of warriors surges down the slope, and everything becomes a blur of movement, noise, and fear.

Rory darts forward to intercept the first wave. I try to follow, truly I do, but a knot of MacIntyre fighters crashes between us, blades flashing. I'm forced back by sheer force of numbers, my sword up, boots skidding on the loose dirt. I lose sight of him almost instantly.

A man swings for my head. I duck, retaliate, steel biting through his side. Another lunges from behind. I twist just in time, catch his wrist, and slam the hilt of my sword into his jaw. He drops. I'm breathing hard already, my heart pounding.

All around me, MacRae men shout battle cries. I scan desperately for Rory, but the field is a churning mass of bodies, and he's nowhere.

Another attacker. Then another. I fight them off, but each blow pushes me farther away from where I started. The more I move, the harder it is to go back.

Someone grabs my braid. I whip around and stab, the blade sinking deep into a man's stomach. He collapses, dragging me down with him. I wrench free and scramble upright, gasping, blood on my hands, tunic, and boots.

Still no Rory and still no way back to the top of the ridge. So I do what I've been taught. I fight. I survive. I try to hold the line and fight my way to the flank where the Lennox banner blows proudly.

The further into the valley I move, the more my boots slip in blood and mud, but I keep my stance low and steady, just like Rory taught me. My sword finds the ribs of a man lunging toward me, and I twist hard before tearing it free. Another comes from behind, but I sense him before I see him, and I pivot, ducking low and slicing his thigh. He topples with a grunt, and I drive my blade into his chest.

All around me, the clash of swords, the thud of bodies hitting the ground, the snarl of warriors, and yet I think of Rory. I hear his voice in my head, teaching me how to disarm someone bigger, how to use their weight against them. How to move my feet constantly. All of his lessons live in my bones now.

A man charges me. Taller, stronger, but slower. I sidestep, slash low, then high, slicing across his face. He roars and grabs blindly for me. I spin and drive my heel into his knee. He crumples. My sword answers with a fatal strike before he can rise.

The world narrows to motion and instinct. I can't afford to think about where I am anymore. I only care where they are, those trying to kill me.

Another approaches, swinging wild, heavier than me by three times. I block, the force jarring my arms, but I use his momentum to wrench the blade from his grip. He backs away too late. I lunge. His throat opens like parchment.

Blood mists the air. My arms ache. There's a cut across my bicep I hadn't noticed until it starts to sting, and another on my hip. Shallow, but raw.

Still, I fight.

They don't expect it from me. A woman. Small and quick. I see it in their eyes every time they hesitate, and I use that hesitation to end them.

I don't know how far I've gone. I can't even see the MacRae banner anymore. Just hills, smoke, and enemies that seem endless.

Eventually, they begin to break, and the tide shifts. Our warriors press forward, and the MacIntyre forces begin to scatter, disorganized, some screaming for retreat. I watch as they run, boots pounding over the valley. It should be a relief, but I don't see Rory any more.

I'm alone.

Breathing hard, I turn in a slow circle. The trees here are unfamiliar. The slopes are steeper. The ridge I started near is completely out of sight. I can't hear Rory's voice. I can't hear Duncan shouting. Just the wind and the moans of dying men.

How far did I travel?

I stagger a few steps forward, blood seeping from my hip now. Not bad, certainly not deadly, but it hurts. My arms feel like heavy stones, and my legs tremble beneath me. Still, I walk.

The castle is somewhere behind me. I just need to find my bearings. I start up the nearest hill, hoping the height will help me orient myself. But then I hear it: the clink of armor, the crunch of boots on loose rock. I freeze. My grip tightens on the hilt as I raise my blade and brace, my heart hammering in my chest.

And then I see him.

Lachlan.

He's calm, almost smug, as if the blood around us is beneath his notice. His cloak is unsoiled, and his hair is tied back neatly. He's flanked by two men I don't recognize.

"What do you want?" I growl, my blade still raised.

He gives me a mock bow. "You, of course."

"I'm not yours to take."

"That's what they all say, but today you're wrong."

The men move to grab me, but I lash out before they can close the distance. I catch one in the shoulder, but a blow to the back of my head knocks me to my knees, dizzy. I drop my sword when a boot presses hard against my back.

"Bind her," Lachlan says coolly. "Gently. She's no use to me dead."

I snarl and twist, biting the hand that grabs me, but they overpower me and wind rope around my wrists.

Lachlan crouches, his face too close. "You're a warrior now, Cait. I'll grant you that. But I'll warn you—you will be my wife, or you will never be seen or heard from again."

"You'll never get away with this."

"I already have."

They haul me upright, shoving me onto Lachlan's horse. I can't even see the battlefield anymore.

"Let's go," he says, and they drag me toward Drummond lands.

We ride until the last of the sun slips from the sky. My wrists burn from the rope, and my arms go numb from being behind my back. I'm exhausted and have been bleeding from my hip for hours. The clang of steel still echoes in my ears. Blood still streaks my skin, and I don't know if Rory or Duncan are alive or dead.

I lift my head just enough to see dark hills I don't recognize rolling past us. We are too far from the MacRae border, and too close to Drummond. Every step the horse takes carries me further from my home, and from Rory. My chest aches, my wounds sting, but I don't let myself cry.

"You're quiet," Lachlan says, glancing back at me with a smirk. "That's not like you."

I say nothing.

"Don't worry. You'll be back in a proper castle soon."

"Untie me and we'll see how quiet I stay," I mutter.

He laughs, low and cruel. "Ah, there's the fire I remember." He slows the horse just a little. "You've made it far too easy, Cait. Once you marry me, the councils will have no choice. They'll give me everything—your land, your holdings—and once the papers are sealed, I'll have what I've wanted all along."

I glare at him. "You'll never get the word of my brother Duncan, or his inheritance. He'd rather raze the land than hand it to a coward like you."

"Oh, I won't ask him," he says, eyes gleaming. "I'll get it from you. You're the heir now, aren't you?"

The breath leaves my lungs like a blow. My heart stutters. "What did you say?" I demand.

He doesn't answer right away, just gives me smug silence. My stomach turns. "Duncan's not dead," I snap. "He's not. You're lying." But my voice cracks on the last word. I bite it back, gripping the saddle tighter.

I can't afford to fall apart. Not now. Not until I know. Not until I see him with my own eyes. But the image rises anyway. Duncan on the battlefield, bleeding and alone, and I have to blink hard to force it away. "If you've touched him," I hiss, "if you've hurt my brother, I swear I'll see you burn."

Lachlan's response is slow and cruel. "That's exactly what's happened. Your brother was too much trouble. Brave, I'll give him that, but not quite brave enough."

"You bastard!"

"Now, now," he cuts in, arrogant as ever. "You should be thanking me. With Duncan out of the way, that makes you heir to everything. And I've got a priest waiting at my castle as we speak. We'll be wed by midnight, and I'll own the MacRae lands *and* my father's. No one will rival me in the Highlands." He leans closer. "All you have to do, Cait, is smile and play the bride."

His words hit me like a hammer to the chest. Lachlan—*Lachlan*—started this whole nightmare. The battle, the bloodshed, the ruin... it was all his doing. My father, my mother, Duncan—they're gone because of him. Because of *his* greed. Suddenly the world feels too heavy to carry.

My hands tremble, and tears burn behind my eyes, but anger rises faster, a slow, fierce flame kindling deep in my chest. Lachlan took everything—*my* family—and I will not let him have the last word. I won't bow to this monster.

Clenching my fists, I glare at him. "You will pay for this," I hiss, my voice low and hard. "I swear on my blood, Lachlan—you will regret the day you set your hand against the MacRaes." The fire in me roars, drowning out the sorrow for a moment. He may have started this war, but I will finish it.

They stop when one of Lachlan's men slumps from his saddle with a grunt, clutching his chest. Blood darkens his tartan. The others dismount quickly, tearing strips of cloth for bandages.

Lachlan hauls me off his horse. My whole body aches, and my wrists are raw, but I stand.

He looks calm, and pleased. "I had eyes on you the entire battle," he says. "Scouts on the ridge line, tracking your every move."

My stomach turns. "You had me followed?"

"I made sure you weren't lost in the fray. Couldn't let my prize get away, could I?"

"You planned this," I say slowly. "Everything."

He smiles like it's a compliment. "Of course. Stir up an old border feud, send a few men to provoke yours into battle."

"Duncan," I whisper, my throat tightening.

"I had my strongest man kill him."

I stagger back a step. "You killed my brother."

He doesn't deny it. "He was in my way."

"And my parents?" I ask. "Was it your men who took them?"

His expression doesn't change. "Of course. The plan was to take you too, force you all into signing over your hand and your land, but the imbeciles didn't bring you back to me."

I can barely breathe. "The village," I say. "That was all your idea too?"

He tilts his head. "I burned it. Couldn't risk your father gathering support. Easier to burn the whole thing, and I knew it would draw you out of the woods, Caitriona."

I can taste the grief on my tongue. "So you slaughtered my family, and you still think I'm going to marry you?"

"You will," he says, stepping closer. "Once we're wed, I'll hold more land than any other laird in the Highlands. Your father's land. Mine. All of it."

"There's no priest on earth who could make me your wife."

"There's one waiting at my castle. He doesn't need your consent. Only your presence."

Rage coils in my chest, sharp and searing. "I would rather die."

Lachlan's gaze narrows, but I see the flicker behind it. A sliver of doubt.

I may be bound, bloodied, and alone. But I'm not broken. Not yet.

CHAPTER 23

The forest swallows sound. Only the wind moves, brushing the treetops and rattling leaves, and the only light is from the moon and stars. I'm thankful for the bright full moon as I press forward, my eyes scanning every track, every broken branch. Cait's out here, somewhere.

If Cait had died on that field, I'd know. I've looked at every face, every broken body left behind when the fighting stopped. I searched through every blood-soaked and torn tartan. I looked under every shattered shield, lifted limbs and turned over corpses until my hands shook. And she wasn't there. She's not among the dead. I'd feel it if she were. Something in me would break beyond repair. No, she's alive. She has to be.

If she isn't dead, then she's been taken, and there's only one man who would dare. Lachlan. The thought settles like ice in my gut. With the chaos of battle masking his treachery, he'd have the perfect cover to carry her away.

If he's laid a hand on her, if he's dragged her anywhere against her will, I'll find him. And I'll make him wish he'd died on the field instead.

I crest the hill and freeze. There's a man below, slumped beside a stream with the Drummond banner tied around his horse. I can tell from the way he's leaning over that he's wounded. His sword is nearby, and his horse is well fed, strong and steady.

I could walk away. Let the man live. Keep searching on foot like I've been doing. But I'm running out of time. If Cait is out there, every hour I waste on foot gives Lachlan more time to hurt her. I don't want to kill a man for a horse, but if I don't, and Cait suffers for it, I'll never forgive myself.

The horse is tethered just loosely enough for a quick getaway. I stay hidden as I move closer, my heart pounding.

I drop low, weight forward, every inch of my body and mind alert. The slope beneath me is steep, but I've got gravity on my side. I breathe through my nose, slow and shallow, my heart thudding in my ears. I've trained for this. Step, settle, scan. I roll each step heel to toe, placing my boots where the moss is thickest and the branches thinnest. No snapping twigs. No clumsy slides. My fingers skim the ground for balance, and I keep to the tree shadows, watching the lone warrior the whole time.

I stay low, inching closer with each silent breath. The man hasn't seen me. It's just the three of us—him, me, and the horse that's about to carry me to Cait.

I rise in a slow crouch, my grip tightening on the hilt of my blade. One step more and I'm behind him. His head is turned the other way, and he never hears me.

I grab him by the cloak, yanking him backward hard. He chokes out a sound, a half gasp, half warning, but it's cut short the instant my blade draws across his throat. Hot blood spills over my hand, and his body convulses once before going limp.

I shove him to the ground, already reaching for the horse's rope before the beast can spook. The mare shudders, her ears flicking, but I whisper low and steady as I catch the reins. "Easy. You're mine now."

I pull the Drummond banner off the horse and swing into the saddle before the man's body even stops twitching. There's no time for guilt. This horse might be the only reason I reach Cait before Lachlan does whatever vile thing he's planned.

I spur the horse south toward the edge of Drummond land, blood still wet on my hands. I don't feel the gash along my ribs anymore, nor the stiffness in my shoulder. Only the ache in my chest. An ache that's grown sharper with every moment since I lost sight of Cait in the chaos.

We had a plan. We were meant to fight side by side. Stay close. I'd said those words. "Stay close. Stay safe." And then she was gone, swallowed by the attack.

A flash of light catches my eye, small and glinting in the moonlight at the foot of a pine. I kneel and lift it gently from the grass. I dismount, holding the reins tightly.

Her comb.

Not just any comb, but the one her father carved for her mother. Cait wore it on her belt this morning, tucked tight against her hip for good fortune.

The ground near the comb is scuffed with hoof prints and boot marks tangled together with faint smears of blood. A trail, not just of movement, but of struggle.

"She was here," I whisper, closing my fingers around the comb. "I'm coming, Cait."

I start following the trail, scanning for more signs. I barely make it a hundred yards before I spot movement ahead. Men in Lennox tartan, dismounted and moving through the undergrowth with caution.

One of them spots me and raises his blade, but I hold up my hands.

"MacRae," I say, panting. "I'm looking for Lady Caitriona."

Without hesitation, the Lennox man nods. "Come. You'll ride with us."

Cait is fierce. She would not be easy to capture, but if they've hurt her—no. I can't let myself think about it. She's alive. She has to be.

A few miles more, we see trampled grass and bloodied bandages abandoned beside a fallen log.

"They stopped here," one of the men says. "Someone was bleeding bad."

I dismount and kneel. The blood's still wet.

Please, not hers.

I rise slowly, my jaw clenched. "They're not far."

The Lennox men ready their weapons, quiet and grim. They're good fighters. Loyal. We push on, the terrain growing steeper as we cross into Drummond land.

The ridge gives us the perfect vantage. I spot them first. Three riders crossing the open meadow below, moonlight glinting off their weapons and polished saddles. My chest goes tight the moment I see her.

Cait.

She's slumped in front of Lachlan on his horse, her hands bound behind her back, her posture stiff with pain or exhaustion—probably both. Her hair's tangled, her clothes streaked with blood and dirt. But she's alive. I feel it like a thunderclap in my chest.

"There," I say, pointing. "That's them."

The Lennox men draw in beside me, their expressions darkening. "Aye," one mutters. "Drummond bastard's gotten bold."

I keep my eyes locked on the trio. "Do any of you have a throwing axe?"

One of the men nods, pulls a short-handled axe from the loop on his belt, and hands it over. The weight of it feels good in my palm. Solid. Sharp. Balanced.

"I'll take the men flanking him," I say. "You all ride ahead, cut Lachlan off. Get in front of him and make him stop."

They don't hesitate, riding at full speed, angling around the meadow to intersect Lachlan's path. I press my heels to my horse's sides and charge.

My hand tightens on the axe. I rise slightly in the stirrups, draw my arm back—and let it fly.

The blade spins end over end, a flash of steel against the sky—then lands with a dull thunk in the forehead of the man riding to Lachlan's right. He drops instantly, toppling backward off his saddle.

The second rider turns his horse around, his eyes wide as he sees me bearing down. I don't slow. Instead, I veer to the left at the last second, rising in the stirrups and leaping from my saddle straight onto his. The impact knocks him sideways, and before he can recover, I drive my dagger up beneath his ribs, straight into his heart. He chokes on a gasp, his eyes going glassy, and I shove him off the horse. His body hits the ground hard, rolling limp through the grass.

I turn, now on foot, to see Lachlan's grip on Cait tighten, his face twisted in fury.

But it's too late.

The Lennox riders thunder in from the opposite direction and form a wall in front of him, their horses shoulder to shoulder, blocking the way. Lachlan's horse skids to a halt, rearing slightly, and he curses, scrambling for control.

I sprint to where the Lennox men have Lachlan trapped. They've formed a tight circle around him, horses snorting and stamping as they hold him in place like wolves closing in on wounded prey. One of them dismounts without a word, grabs Lachlan by the collar, and yanks him down from the saddle. He crashes to the ground with a grunt, dust and leaves flying up around him—just as I reach them.

I don't hesitate. Rage drives me forward like a hammer. I slam my boot into his chest, knocking the wind from him, and he gasps like a man drowning, his arms scrabbling against the earth.

I want to slaughter him then and there, end it with my blade and be done, but I force myself to step back. I let the Lennox lads rough him up, let him feel the weight of what he's done. I turn instead to the one thing that matters. I help Cait off Lachlan's horse, her face pale and drawn, wrists bound and raw. My hands tremble as I draw my blade, but I'm careful, gentle, when I cut the ropes. Her arms fall forward, shaking, red marks like welts around her skin. She sways, and I catch her before she can fall, pulling her tight into my chest. She sags against me, her breath hitching, but she's breathing. She's here, and I'll never let her go again.

Cait lifts her face, her eyes tear filled yet fierce. "I knew you'd find me," she whispers, her voice rough from exhaustion.

I brush a strand of hair from her cheek, my thumb lingering there. "And I knew you'd survive," I say, letting out a shaky breath and pressing my forehead to hers. "You're safe now. I promise."

The Lennox men keep Lachlan on his knees, blood dripping from his nose, his hands bound tight behind him now with the same rope he used on Cait. He spits blood onto the grass and glares up at me like I'm the one who wronged *him*.

I look Cait in the eye and ask, "How do you want to kill him?"

She doesn't flinch. Doesn't blink. Just steps forward, slow and steady, until she's standing right in front of him.

"With my father's sword," she says.

I nod once, hand her Laird MacRae's sword, and step aside. The Lennox men shove Lachlan to his knees before Cait.

Lachlan begs for his life.

"I had to bury my mother and father after you murdered them. You killed my brother!" she screams, her voice shaking with rage.

She raises the blade, fury radiating off her in waves. But just before the steel touches Lachlan's throat, I step forward.

"Wait," I say, my voice low but firm. "Duncan isn't dead."

Cait freezes, her chest heaving. Her grip on the sword loosens, just slightly.

I keep my voice steady, calm. "I killed the man who attacked him. Duncan was bleeding, but he's alive."

She stares at me like she's trying to piece the world back together.

And then—she laughs.

Right in Lachlan's face.

A sharp, bitter sound, full of shock and relief, her shoulders shaking with it.

"You really are pathetic," she tells Lachlan, her voice hoarse but strong. "You can't even get murder right."

His face twists with confusion and pain. Cait steps closer, crouching in front of him, bloodstained and wild-eyed.

Lachlan tries to speak, but she doesn't let him.

"You're not a warrior. You're not even a leader. You're just a coward who ties up women and hides behind men braver than you'll ever be."

She stands and looks at me, her hand steady once more. "Now I'm ready."

And then—without hesitation—she ends it.

Lachlan collapses into the earth, defeated in every way.

Cait walks back to me.

"I'm here," I whisper, holding her tight. "It's over."

She leans into me. "He won't hurt anyone ever again."

"No," I say. "He won't."

One of the Lennox lads raises his sword to the moonlit sky and shouts, "Long live Lady Caitriona MacRae!"

Another echoes him. "The Highland queen of the north!"

The others take up the chant with rising fervor, clanging sword hilts against shields and saddles, voices ringing across the ridge like a battle hymn. "Lady Caitriona! The MacRae queen!"

Cait stands breathless beside me, her face flushed with cold and adrenaline, the blood on her hands drying into stiff patches. But there's pride in her posture now—no shame, no trembling.

One of the older Lennox men rides up beside us and dips his head with something close to awe. "We'll be setting up camp just north of here before midnight," he says. "Too dark to ride much further. The land turns to Lennox territory in a few leagues."

He glances toward the trees. "You two ought to take a quieter path, just the pair of you. You'll draw less attention that way."

Another rider nods. "Head due north. If you do, you'll pass through Gibbons land before dawn. There's a healer who lives there. She is strange and lives alone in the woods, but she's kind. Folks say she can mend any wound."

I thank them both, but before we ride on, the lad who lent me his throwing axe strides toward the dead Drummond man. With a grunt, he yanks his weapon free from the man's skull, wipes the blade on the grass, and turns to me.

"I've seen a lot in battle," he says, panting slightly. "But I've *never,*

ever, seen a throw like that, and in the dark? How do you even train for that?"

I give him a nod. "Thank you. For the axe."

He grins, tosses it once in his hand like it weighs nothing. "Aye, it was worth it to see that."

We part ways at the fork in the ridge. The Lennox lads head northeast to make camp. Cait and I turn our horses northwest, riding into the moonlight.

Toward home. Toward healing.

CHAPTER 24

Moonlight leads us forward, casting silver streams of light across the hills. My wrists ache from the ropes, and my hip throbs with each step my horse takes, but we can't stop. Not while I can still hear the echo of Lachlan's voice in my head. Not while the night feels fragile, like peace that could break if we breathe too loudly. There could be more enemy stragglers out here, and the risk is too great.

Rory rides beside me, his arm stiff against his body. He hasn't spoken much since we left the Lennox lads, but his eyes find mine often. There's something in them I can't name. Fierce and comforting at once. Something that steadies me better than any words would.

Dawn comes slow, a faint blush against the sky. We find a cave just after the sun peeks above the trees, a hollow tucked into a mossy ridge, hidden by thick pines. It smells of earth and old stone. We tether the horses nearby, and I follow Rory inside, stumbling a little on the uneven ground, exhausted.

"I've got you," he murmurs, catching my elbow gently, his touch careful around the bruises.

He lowers himself with a wince, favoring his ribs, and I kneel beside him, my teeth clenched against the pull in my hip. Neither of us says the obvious: that we shouldn't be moving like this, that we need a healer and a full week of sleep. Yet we only have each other, and for now, that's enough.

We lie down on cloaks and saddle blankets layered across the stone floor, shoulder to shoulder. My body aches, but warmth spreads between us as Rory tugs me close.

His breath brushes the crown of my head. "You're safe," he whispers.

"We're safe," I echo, pressing my cheek to his chest, right where his heart beats slow and steady beneath my hand.

We fall asleep in one another's arms.

INSIDE THE CAVE IS QUIET, THE HUSH BROKEN ONLY BY THE SOFT RUSTLE of wind beyond the entrance. Outside, a bird calls once, then falls silent. The sky beyond the mouth of the cave is dusky blue.

We must have slept for hours, curled against the cold stone, wrapped in cloaks and each other.

I shift slightly, my muscles aching from the battle, the ride, and everything that's come before and after. The motion stirs the warmth between us, and I reach for Rory. My fingers find his face in the half-light, cool at first, then warm as I trace the line of his jaw.

He stirs beneath my touch, his eyes opening slowly.

"Good morrow," I whisper.

He blinks, his eyes finding mine in the dim morning light. Then his hand finds my waist, gentle and slow. "I was dreaming of you," he says, voice low.

"You're not dreaming now," I whisper.

He leans in brushing his lips to mine, soft and reverent, like he's still half-asleep and not entirely sure I'm real. But I am. And he is. And when I kiss him back, my hand sliding to the nape of his neck, there's no more doubt between us.

We kiss slowly, our bodies learning new shapes around pain and exhaustion. His good hand slides to my breasts, and I inhale sharply, not from fear, but need and ache.

"I don't want to hurt you," he murmurs.

"You won't," I whisper, and I mean it. I tug at his shirt gently, revealing the wound along his ribs. He winces as I skim my fingers over the bruises, but he doesn't stop me.

His hands move to my belt, hesitating as he brushes the cut above my hip. "Tell me if anything hurts."

"I will."

We undress each other slowly. He kisses every inch of skin he uncovers, like it deserves to be honored.

When he finally enters me, it's careful. No thrusting, just slow, deep, strokes. A deliciously slow joining; a surrender. His forehead rests against mine, and our breathing falls into a rhythm. We move together as if we've done this a hundred times. I feel the pain in my body fade behind the rising warmth between us, as if love could heal in ways medicine cannot.

There are no words, only the softness of our mouths, the press of our hands, the trembling release of what we've carried too long.

Afterward, we stay tangled together, skin warm against skin, our breath slowing. My hip aches again, but I don't care.

Rory kisses my shoulder, then my temple. "You're everything," he says, his voice rough with sleep and love.

"You're my everything too," I say, and I've never known anything with such fierce certainty.

I close my eyes and draw him nearer. For a while, we lie still, wrapped in each other and in silence, before rising to see to the horses and continue the journey home.

By mid-day, the pain in my hip sharpens into a steady throb with every step. Rory helps me onto the horse's back, his jaw tight as he suppresses a wince from his own injuries. His shirt is damp with sweat despite the chill in the air, and I can tell the ride will cost us both. Still, we press on. Neither of us says it aloud, but we're too far from home to risk illness. We need help. A proper healer. Somewhere safe.

The sun is high by the time we reach Gibbons territory, the trees thinner here, the terrain more familiar. I know this forest, though not well. They border my family's holdings, but we've never had cause to visit this neck of the woods.

Rory slows his mount as a narrow path emerges from the brush. "There," he says, pointing.

I follow his gaze. A stone chimney rises behind a thicket of rowan trees, which are said to be used for protection and the connection between spiritual realms. A cottage, low and ivy covered, nearly disappears into the land around it. Smoke curls lazily from the chimney.

We dismount, stiff and sore. Rory ties the horses near a patch of tall grass, and I limp beside him as we approach the door. Before we can knock, it opens.

She stands in the doorway like she's been waiting for us, a young woman, not much older than me, with dark curls that tumble past her shoulders and bright eyes the color of moss after rain. A worn green cloak is fastened at her neck with a carved wooden brooch.

Rory stops short, his breath catching. "Fiona?"

The name hits me like a splash of cold water. I stare at him, my heart pounding. *Fiona*. That was the name he called me the day we met, before he knew me. But how could he know anyone by that name, anyone from this time, from this land, when he's not even from here? He's from another world, *and* another century. Yet he said it like it meant something. Like she meant something….

The woman smiles softly. "No, sorry," she says. "I'm called *Mairen*. You must've known someone who looks like me then?"

Rory blinks, stunned. "You look—just exactly like her… I'm sorry, Miss." He stops himself.

Mairen's gaze flicks to me. "You're both hurt."

I nod, suddenly dizzy. "Aye. I'm Cait and this is Rory. We need help, we beg of ye."

Without hesitation, she steps aside and motions us in. "Then come inside, and let's see what can be mended."

The cottage has a stunning, vibrant purple bush near the front door, its sweet scent wrapping around me like a soft cloak. I glance up at Mairen. "What kind of bush is that?"

She smiles gently. "That's lilac, m'lady. A healer's friend, its scent wards off ill spirits and soothes the weary."

Inside, Mairen's cottage smells of lilac, thyme, and smoke, sweet and earthy. Dried herbs hang from the beams above us—lavender, sage, rosemary—while jars line the shelves along the far wall, labeled in a spidery hand. A kettle simmers over the fire, and the table is already set with bread, honey, and a bowl of berries.

"Sit," Mairen says gently, and we do.

She moves quickly, pouring cups of water from a stone jug and setting them in front of us. I drink greedily, letting it cool the ache in my throat. Rory watches her closely, as though trying to reconcile her face with a ghost.

"What happened to you both?" she asks as she gathers clean cloth and a jar of golden salve.

"There was a battle, then I was captured," I say, gulping more water between thoughts. "Rival clan. He saved my life."

"And she saved mine," Rory adds, giving me a look that lingers.

Mairen hums low in her throat. "Hmm. Sounds like the kind of story that leaves a mark."

She starts with Rory. His ribs are mottled purple and black, and he hisses as she unwinds the old bandage. "Breathe through it," she murmurs, smoothing the salve over the bruising in delicate circles.

"You have a light hand," he says through gritted teeth.

She smiles. "That's the idea." When she finishes binding his chest, she tends to the cut on his arm, dabbing it clean before stitching it with a curved bone needle. Rory doesn't flinch.

Then it's my turn.

Mairen helps me onto the bed near the hearth and carefully lifts the hem of my tunic. The gash along my hip is swollen and angry.

"This should've been treated long ago," she mutters, but there's no judgment in her tone, only concern.

She works in silence, her hands sure. The salve she uses is cool and stings only briefly before relief floods the wound.

"What is that?" I ask.

"Comfrey, marigold, a bit of yarrow," she says. "For healing, and to keep the rot away."

She covers the cut with fresh linen and helps me sit up slowly. "Rest now. You'll both be sore for days, but you'll mend."

I glance at Rory, who's already watching me. His eyes are softer now, the tension easing from his shoulders. We're not safe yet, not truly, but this feels like the first step toward it.

Mairen pours more water, then adds hot broth from the kettle. "Eat something," she says, "then sleep. The worst is behind you."

Though it's midday, we fall asleep quickly.

WE MUST HAVE SLEPT ALL NIGHT. THE SOFT LIGHT OF MORNING SLIPS through the small windows as I stir awake. Rory's breath is even beside me, though his arm and ribs still pull at him with every rise and fall of his chest. Mairen is already in the kitchen, her gentle footsteps and quiet humming carrying through the cottage walls.

When we step into the kitchen, she greets us with warm smiles and sets two steaming mugs of chamomile tea before us. The scent is soothing. I take a careful sip, feeling the warmth calm the ache in my body and the nervous tightness in my chest.

"Drink slow," Mairen says kindly. "This'll ease your spirit."

Next, she brings out a bowl of thick, rich stew, fragrant with herbs and tender meat, and a loaf of crusty bread, still warm. The food smells heavenly, and as I tear into the bread, I feel my spirits renew.

Rory leans toward Mairen, his voice soft. "There's a lass back home who looks and sounds just like you, Mairen. I'd wager you two would have been friends, if you'd met Fiona."

I glance at Rory, surprised by the tenderness in his eyes. His words are simple, but they carry no falsehood. He must hold a genuine friendship in his heart for Fiona. Perhaps this tangled weave of past and present, of names whispered and faces remembered, runs deeper and more mysterious than we imagine.

She braids lilacs into my hair, refuses any coin and only asks that we keep her name to ourselves. "Some folks don't much trust women who know how to sew up flesh and talk to crows," she says with a wink, slipping us a large bundle of dried herbs, tied with a thin leather cord. "This will ease your brother's pain and help his wound mend faster," she says softly.

I stare at her, surprised. "How did ye know about my brother? I never spoke of him to ye."

A gentle smile curls her lips. "Ye talk in yer sleep, Lady Cait. Pain slips out when the mind rests."

I clasp Mairen's hands gently. "Thank ye for all ye've done."

Rory nods in thanks as well. With a final smile, we bid Mairen farewell, the promise of home calling us onward.

We leave Mairen's cottage with full bellies, wrapped wounds, and satchels full of jerky and oatcakes. The air is cool, the morning sun bleeding gold into the mist that clings low over the Gibbons land. My horse walks steady beneath me, careful as if she senses my pain, and Rory rides beside me. We ride slow, speaking little. Every jolt and sway sends an ache through my hip, but I grit my teeth and bear it.

My thoughts drift to Duncan.

"Do you think he's alive?" I ask quietly, not looking at Rory.

He doesn't answer right away. I can feel him weighing his words.

"I think so," he says finally. "His wound was deep, but I got him to a wagon and they promised to head straight to the surgeon. Duncan's strong. Stubborn as sin. If anyone could make it through, it's him."

I nod, but it's not enough. I want proof. I want to see my brother's eyes open and hear his whistle again, that whistle he's always used to find me or warn me since we were bairns.

The hills begin to rise, the trees thickening as we near the edge of my family's land. I recognize the path ahead now, an old hunting trail.

I press my hand over my side, feeling the firmly wrapped linen beneath my tunic. Every inch of me throbs, but I refuse to rest again until I see that he's safe. If he's alive, he'll be at the castle. If he's not….

No. I can't finish the thought.

"We're close," I say, scanning the tree line. "Should be able to see the towers by dusk, if we keep a steady pace. Do you think anyone will believe us?"

"They'll believe you," he says. "You're the laird's sister."

"That didn't stop Lachlan from trying to use me like a pawn."

"No. But it means your word holds weight. And you're not alone anymore."

I glance at him, his handsome face shadowed beneath the hood of his cloak, the stubble on his jaw darker than usual.

"I don't know what will happen next," I admit.

"We ride to your family," he says. "We tell them the truth. About the attack. About what Lachlan did. About us."

"Us?"

His eyes meet mine. "Yes. Us. If we can stand side by side in battle and take down Lachlan together, then there's nothing we can't face. We belong together."

"Us," I repeat, and this time there's no question.

We ride on into the growing light, the wind lifting strands of my hair. The road ahead is still uncertain, still dangerous. But with every step, I feel the burden of fear growing lighter, replaced by something fierce and quiet.

Hope.

We reach the gates just before dusk. The sight of the MacRae banner, torn but still flying, brings a lump to my throat I can't swallow. Smoke curls from the watchtower chimney. The drawbridge is lowered. Two guards spot us and rush forward, one shouting for help when he sees the blood on Rory's tunic and the bruises on my face.

We both dismount, and I nearly collapse, but Rory catches me. We stagger into the courtyard.

"Duncan," I rasp. "Where's Duncan?"

A healer hurries to me.

"My brother. Please."

The woman points toward the east wing. "He's alive. Barely slept. Keeps asking after you."

Rory and I run as fast as two battered souls can manage, each stride laced with pain, but neither of us willing to slow down.

I ease open the door to Duncan's chamber, my heart lodged in my throat. The scent of blood lingers, mingling with the sharp tang of herbs. He looks pale against the linens, wrapped in clean bandages, his breath shallow but steady. A fire crackles in the hearth, casting a warm glow over the dark blue bruises along his jaw. He stirs, just barely, and his eyes blink open. When they meet mine, something inside me loosens. "Duncan," I breathe, stepping closer. "You stubborn fool... you're alive." My voice trembles.

"Cait?"

I drop to my knees and throw my arms around him, careful not to jostle his wounds. "I thought you were—"

"I'm not," he murmurs, his hand settling clumsily on my back. "Thanks to Rory."

I pull back and study him. His eyes are ringed with pain, but they're open. I manage a shaky laugh and brush his hair back from his forehead. "You look terrible."

"You smell worse," Duncan mutters, his voice hoarse but teasing. The three of us laugh, even though it aches. Rory curls slightly with a hand over his ribs, Duncan bites back a groan, and I feel the pull of pain along my hip, but we don't stop.

The laughter hurts, but it's the best pain I've ever felt. We're alive. Together. And for this moment, that's enough.

By nightfall, the MacRae warriors and the allied clans gather in the hall. Torches burn bright, casting flickering shadows on faces still streaked with soot and sweat. Every bench is full, warriors shoulder to shoulder, and even those with arms in slings or heads wrapped in bandages sit up straighter when Duncan speaks.

He has to stay seated, but lifts his voice strong and clear.

"You all fought like devils," he begins, looking out at them. "You stood your ground when MacIntyre and Drummond came for our lands. You protected our home."

A murmur of agreement rises from the crowd.

"Lachlan is dead," Duncan says. "Struck down not by fate, but by the will of those he betrayed, and Lady Caitriona's sword. This fight wasn't about pride. It was about greed. About hunger for power that didn't belong to him."

He looks around slowly, his eyes locking with men from every clan: MacRae, Boyd, Gibbons, Campbell, Graham, MacLeod, MacLellon, and MacNab. "We bled together. And we won. But don't let that fool you into thinking the danger's past."

Heads nod. The tension ripples through the room like wind over grass.

"Lachlan may be gone, but his allies live on. Men like him, who take what they want and burn what they can't have, are still out there. They'll return, and I'll be ready. We'll be ready," Duncan says, straightening despite the wince that crosses his face. "If any of you are willing to stand beside me again, then I swear this land—our land—will never fall."

The hall erupts in sound—boots pounding the floor, fists slamming the tables, a chorus of voices shouting *MacRae! MacRae!*

The battle was fierce and unforgiving, yet here we stand—Duncan, Rory, and I—scarred but alive. We are bound by bloodshed, and unyielding hope.

CHAPTER 25

Three days after the battle

I hear the faint laughter of bairns from outside the Lennox family home. Rory reaches the door first and knocks. My heart pounds as we wait. How do you tell someone their world has ended?

Maisy opens the door with baby Leana on her hip and flour on her apron. Her eyes brighten when she sees us, then narrow in confusion.

"Cait. Rory." She shifts the baby to her other hip. "Is Ewan with you?"

The question cleaves straight through me. I glance at Rory, who swallows hard, his jaw tight. I take a deep breath, step forward, and rub her arm.

"Maisy… may we come in?"

Her eyes search our faces. She knows. Not everything, not yet—but enough. Still, she nods and steps back to let us pass.

The house is cramped, warm with the smell of fresh bread. Gavin and Hamish, who are three and four, sit cross-legged on the floor, carving small figures from wood. They look up with bright eyes, hopeful.

Rory crouches by them, his voice gentle. "Would you lads mind playing outside for a wee bit? Just for a moment."

They go without fuss. Maisy sets Leana down in a cradle by the hearth, straightens, and folds her arms across her chest. "Tell me," she says, her voice cracking.

I step closer, reach for her hand, and find it cold. "Maisy… Ewan fought bravely, but he—he won't be coming home."

She stares at me like I've spoken in a language she doesn't understand. Then slowly, her shoulders fall. "No," she says. "No. Not my Ewan."

"I'm so sorry," I whisper.

Maisy's face crumples, and a deep, guttural wail bursts from her throat—raw and wrenching, unlike any sob or cry I've ever heard. It echoes through the house, sharp and desperate, as if her very soul is breaking apart.

Her knees buckle, and she sinks to the cold stone floor, clutching her chest like she's trying to hold what's been ripped from her insides.

Rocking back and forth in pure, unfiltered grief, her raw howls of loss shake me to my core. Rory and I stand frozen, watching her anguish pour out, helpless but present, offering what small comfort we can, simply by being near.

Rory helps her up. "You will not face this alone," he says. "We came to bring you home, to the castle."

Maisy blinks, as though waking. "The castle?"

"There's room," I tell her. "Warm beds. A safe place for the bairns. You'll have everything you need. We love you, Maisy. You are and always have been family."

At first, she doesn't respond. Then she nods once, slowly. "Aye," she says hoarsely. "Help me tell them, and help me pack up our things?"

The younger bairns don't fully understand, and the older ones cry with their whole little bodies. Maisy moves like she's made of glass, careful, fragile, and about to break.

That night, we sleep in the Lennox house. The air is heavy with sorrow, but Maisy's bairns try to rest despite the ache that lingers in their hearts.

THE DAY WE BROUGHT MAISY AND HER BAIRNS BACK TO THE CASTLE WAS gray with mist, the air heavy with the scent of rain and pine. Rory rode close beside their wagon the whole way, while I sat with the Lennox clan in silence, her youngest curled against her side. Grief still clung to Maisy and her young, but the bairns' eyes took in the towering walls and flickering torches of the MacRae stronghold with wonder.

In the days that followed, the spirit of the castle shifted. Now, there are more voices in the corridors, more chairs drawn close to the hearth, and with the Lennox bairns among us, a new kind of hope begins to bloom beneath the sorrow.

And then, just a few nights later, Duncan called for a feast, not just to honor our warriors, but to remind us all of what we still have, and of the home we are building together, brick by hard-won brick.

Tonight the great hall glows with firelight, casting flickers across stone walls and long wooden tables laden with food. Roasted boar, root vegetables, rounds of cheese, and fresh oat bread fill the air with warm, hearty scents. Laughter echoes off the rafters as mugs of ale are passed down the rows, the clink of metal cups striking in time with the thrum of celebration.

Rory sits beside me, watching quietly, his eyes bright beneath the torchlight. Across the hall, the warriors of Clan MacRae lean in to hear Duncan speak. Men who are still scraped and scarred from battle, but upright and proud, their loyalty stitched tighter than ever.

Duncan stands at the head of the room, his back straight, a goblet raised in one hand.

"To those who stood beside me," Duncan says, his voice strong enough to quiet the room, "and bled for this land—I thank you."

A murmur of acknowledgment ripples through the crowd.

"You fought not just for stone walls or family names," he continues, "but for the hearts that beat within them. And you fought well. We held what was ours—and we will hold it forever."

Chairs scrape against the floor as the warriors rise to their feet. Someone lets out a sharp cheer, and others follow, raising their cups. Duncan lifts his goblet higher.

"To the strength of our blades," he says, voice steady, "and the loyalty that binds us."

"To Clan MacRae!" they shout in answer.

After the meal, I walk the corridor with Rory's hand warm in mine. Inside the stone walls, there is laughter, music, the slap of bairn's footsteps. Outside, the moon is rising over the hills, and the guards on the walls nod as we pass.

We stroll together, the castle looming behind us, a quiet silhouette against the night sky. I glance over at Rory—his sleeves rolled up, dark hair tousled by the wind, his gaze turned toward the tree line. There are still so many things I'm curious to know about him.

"Rory," I say, my voice careful, "can I ask you something?"

He glances at me and slows his step. "Of course."

"Who was Fiona?"

He stops walking, and chuckles softly. "She was a friend."

"Were you in love with her?"

He shakes his head, smiling. "No. We were never like that. Fiona was a historian on the movie set. The one I was working on before I… landed here."

I blink. "A historian?"

"Yes. She knew everything there was to know about Highland clans, especially yours. She said your clan was attacked more than once, but you and Duncan always held your own."

That draws a laugh out of me. "Sounds like Fiona knew us better than we knew ourselves."

Rory's gaze softens. "She certainly respected you."

A strange warmth spreads through my chest, perhaps pride. Or something deeper. "Did you know who I was? Before you came?"

He hesitates, then shakes his head. "No. Not really. Fiona mentioned a sister and brother—defenders of their land, stubborn as hell—but she never gave me names. Just a few details. I didn't know your name is Cait, only that you were from the MacRae family."

He turns toward me, and his voice is softer. "Now I feel like I've known you all my life."

"I feel the same way," I say, heart racing in my chest.

We walk a little farther, the loose stones crunching softly under our boots, until we reach the edge of the path where the orchard meets the stables. Rory stops and turns toward me, both of his hands finding my waist.

His eyes search mine, and I see the truth mirrored in them. "I never believed in fate or destiny, until I met you. I believe in *this*. In you."

I rise onto my toes and kiss him. He responds with a hunger barely restrained, his arms wrapping around me, holding me as though he's afraid I'll vanish if he lets go.

The quiet stables loom behind us, warm, dark, and familiar. I take his hand and tug him toward them, wordless. We slip through the door and into the hay-scented dimness. Moonlight filters in through the high slats, catching in his eyes as he closes the door behind us.

I press my back against the wall, breathless, and he comes to me in the hush, his lips finding mine again—deeper this time, with a tenderness that gives way to need. His hands roam over my waist, my hips, and I tug at his shirt, desperate to feel the heat of him, the solid, steady weight of him grounding me in this moment.

Here, in the quiet shelter of straw and moonlight, we stop thinking. We just feel.

And we don't come apart until the first light of dawn.

CHAPTER 26

Rory

Two weeks later

Maisy and her children live in the warm suite above the kitchens now, where the sun spills in every morning and the fire never goes out. The kids have taken to castle life faster than anyone expected, chasing each other through the corridors, sneaking honeyed oatcakes from the pantry.

Cait says she sees Maisy smile a little more each day. She carries her grief like something sacred, not something shattered. We often find her with her youngest asleep in her arms, staring into the flames with a quiet strength that makes something in my chest ache.

None of us are the same people we were before the battle. Loss has a way of reshaping things. But in the wreckage it left behind, new threads have formed—connections, routines, small joys we didn't expect. Life is stitching itself back together.

The castle breathes again.

Duncan walks without a crutch now. His wounds are healing better than anyone dared hope, though I catch the occasional wince when the weather turns or when he pushes himself too far. He's quieter, more thoughtful. I've seen him standing on the battlements at dawn, watching the hills like they hold answers. Cait remembers their father used to do the same.

Duncan doesn't talk much about the battle or the men we lost, but I can tell it lives inside him now. Every decision he makes carries that weight.

He's a good laird, and the men follow him with quiet respect. He's doubled the guard rotation, ordered every gate checked twice as often, and made sure no one strays far without a weapon. Rival clans may be licking their wounds, but no one here believes they're finished. Even in peace, danger lurks in the background like a distant drumbeat.

And somehow, I've made a place for myself here.

I didn't plan to stay. When I first fell through time, all I could think about was getting home. Back to my time, my job, my apartment with its electricity, running water, and takeout menus. I kept telling myself I'd find a way home.

Now, I wake up to the sound of roosters and the smell of peat smoke. I've got mud on my boots and a dagger on my hip at all times. More importantly, I have a place at the table, and somehow... I fit in.

The people here, their loyalty, the way they *see* and honor one another, stirs something in me. A longing to put down roots, to plant seeds and see what might grow.

Cait's fierceness, fearlessness, and kindness, changed me in ways I still don't fully understand. She makes me want to be braver, and better. She looks at me like I *belong*, and I think maybe I do. I even catch myself saying *ye* instead of *you*, calling a child a *bairn* without thinking.

The truth is, I don't miss the future. Not really. Sometimes I miss the microwave and internet, sure, but not enough to trade this life. Not enough to leave her.

I used to think time travel was a mistake. That I'd fallen through history by accident. But now... I think maybe I was always meant to land here and to find her.

So I've made my choice: I'm staying in the sixteenth century. I'm building something real with my hands, and with my heart. Cait's my home now, and I'd walk through fire or flood to keep her safe and stay by her side.

Most evenings, Cait and I walk the halls together, passing a flask between us, trading stories. Some of them are even true, and some are so ridiculous she narrows her eyes at me until I admit I made them up.

I've taken an interest in one of the wounded boys from the battle. Tavish Graham, barely fourteen, with a chest wound that nearly killed him and eyes that have seen far too much. He's healing now, thanks to Mairen's strange salves and whatever comfort I can offer. I sit with him every day, bring him sweets, tell him stories he pretends not to care about but always listens to.

"My family has a lot of Tavish Grahams in the lineage," I mention to Cait one afternoon after leaving the lad's bedside.

"You think you might be kin?" she teases, smiling.

I nod. "Maybe. Or maybe I just want to believe I have roots here. That I didn't fall into this world by accident."

She takes my hand. "It wasn't by chance, Rory. I truly believe we were meant to find each other."

I don't answer with words. I just pull her close and kiss her.

The morning air bites as I cross the courtyard, sharp enough to sting my cheeks. The castle's more awake than usual with men readying weapons, checking tack, inspecting blades with a silent focus that comes naturally when we smell trouble in the wind. Word of unrest spreads fast in the Highlands.

I find Cait in the solar, bent over a map open on the table between, studying it with Duncan. I join them, my arms folded, looking at the pass she's pointing to.

"This one," she says. "If I were going to attack us, I'd come from here."

"She's right," I say. "It's unguarded, and the trees give too much cover. We can't afford to be surprised."

Duncan rubs his jaw, frowning. "Aye. We've mended, but the clan's still tired from the last fight. Another ambush—"

"We won't let it come to that," Cait cuts in. "We send scouts. Trusted men. Small groups, covering every route."

"And often," I add. "Daily, if we can. Not just to see them coming. To remind them we're watching."

Duncan nods slowly. "I can spare the men. But they'll need to move quietly. No formation, no torches, no smoke."

"I'll go," I say without hesitation. "I can scout. I'm fast, and I know how to move without being seen."

Duncan arches a brow. "You go, but not alone."

"I'll go with him," Cait says before either of us can oppose the idea.

Duncan hesitates a moment. "You can go too, but you stay together," he says.

I glance sideways at her. "He didn't argue. We're making progress," I say with a wink.

"We'll send you east," Duncan says. "North and south will be covered by other groups. Get some volunteers for your party. No one rides alone, no one goes further than a day out. Report back the moment you see anything."

"I'll tell the scouts what to watch for," I say. "Campfire remains, trampled brush, disturbed game trails."

"We leave at dawn," Cait says.

Duncan nods, rising slowly but with more strength than he had last week. "Prepare."

He limps toward the barracks, and Cait and I step out into the courtyard together. The mood has changed. No one's joking now. Men tighten their gear, check their arrows, and move like they expect something.

By sundown, the scouts are chosen, supplies packed, and weapons counted. We ride out at first light. Whatever's waiting, we'll face it together.

WE DIG A SHALLOW PIT TO KEEP THE FIRE LOW. CAIT AND I SIT CLOSE beside it on a saddle blanket, wrapped in cloaks, while four of our best scouts keep watch along the ridge, taking turns, always listening.

She leans back on her elbows, staring up through the branches at the thin slice of moon. I pass her a strip of dried meat, and she takes it with a smile.

"Cait," I say. "Can I ask you something?"

She turns toward me, curious. "Of course."

I shift to face her. Everything slows down. I've thought about this moment so many times it's like I'm walking through a dream I already know by heart.

"I've spent every day since I got here asking why—why this place, this clan... why me... why *you*. But the more time I spend with you, the more I think, no, the more I *know*—it was always you I was being pulled toward. I didn't even know your name before I came through that river, but the more we go through together, the more I see how brave, honorable, kind, and caring you are... Cait, you fight better than any man I know... and you're so stunningly beautiful."

I get up on one knee.

"I don't know how long I'll be in this time—or what's waiting—but I want to face it with you. I want a life here with you. As my beginning and end." I draw the ring from my cloak pocket. It's simple gold but shines in the firelight. "Cait MacRae, will you marry me?"

She presses her hands to her mouth, then laughs, tears spilling. "Yes," she says. "Yes, of course I will."

I slide the ring onto her finger. She flings her arms around me and knocks us both back onto the blanket. We laugh into the kiss, breathless and dizzy.

When we finally pause, her forehead rests against mine. "How long have you been carrying that?" she whispers.

"Since three days after the battle when I asked Duncan if he knew where I could find a ring so I could marry his sister." I laugh.

She sits up, admiring it, handmade, imperfect, and delicate.

"Where did the two of you come up with such a pretty ring?" she asks.

I grin, grateful she likes it. "We had it made for you."

Cait smiles, her eyes a little misty, her cheeks flushed from more than just the cold, and I can't stop looking at her. I can't believe she said yes.

I let out a breath that feels like it's been sitting in my chest for months and laugh, rubbing the back of my neck. "You know what's funny?"

She raises an eyebrow. "What?"

"I never would have imagined I'd propose to my future wife, five hundred years in the past. I always thought if I ever proposed to someone, it'd be in front of thousands of people." I grin, shaking my head. "Like, at a Major League Baseball game, on the jumbotron between innings, or maybe in front of Cinderella's castle at Disney World with fireworks going off behind us."

She blinks at me. "I've gotta be honest with you, Rory... I only understood about half the words you just said."

I laugh again, louder this time, and lean in to kiss her temple. "Yeah, I figured. Sorry. Old habits."

She tilts her head, amused. "What's a jumbotron?"

"Remember how I told you about movies? It's like that but a massive screen. It shows close-ups of sweaty athletes and people proposing marriage while eating overpriced hot dogs."

"And this *Disney World?*"

"It's a pretend magical kingdom, mostly for children and exhausted parents. You'd hate the crowds, but you'd love the roller coasters."

"Roller coasters?"

"Enormous, fast-moving... wagons.... You know what? I'll draw you a picture of one when we get home," I laugh.

She snorts. "You are the strangest man I've ever known."

"And you're the best thing that's ever happened to me," I say softly, tugging her closer.

We see a star shoot through the sky, and the woods around us are quiet. Somehow, right here in the middle of nowhere, it feels like we're outside of time, and like this is exactly where we're meant to be.

CHAPTER 27

My bedchamber smells faintly of lavender and lye soap, and the rushes on the floor have been freshly changed. Maisy stands behind me, fastening the last row of delicate buttons on the back of my velvet gown.

"I can't believe this day has come," she says excitedly.

I meet her gaze in the polished metal mirror propped on the table. "Neither can I."

She smooths the fabric over my shoulders, then brushes a curl back from my cheek. "You look beautiful, Cait."

We had invited the healer Mairen to the wedding, of course, and she'd arrived just before I began dressing with a bundle of freshly cut lilacs in her arms, their scent sweet and sharp in the morning air. "Every bride needs a bit of bloom," she'd said.

Maisy weaves the lilac blossoms into my hair with those careful, clever hands of hers. Next, she moves to the table and picks up my bouquet.

Rory crafted it himself, rising early to choose each flower from the castle gardens and the fields beyond. He wove together white roses, violets, and bluebells, their scents mingling like something both ancient and tender. A few strands of ivy curl through it, green and strong, and at the center he'd placed one perfect, pink, foxglove, sturdy, beautiful, and entirely unexpected. He'd tied it all with white linen. "For love that endures," he wrote on the note.

Outside, I hear the distant clatter of hooves in the courtyard, men calling greetings, the rise of a fiddle warming up. The world is still turning, but mine is changing forever.

"I used to think I'd be married off like a transaction," I say quietly. "To Lachlan or someone like him. Someone who wanted land, not love."

Maisy doesn't answer right away. Then she says, "And instead, you have a tall, handsome warrior who lives and breathes for you. Not a bad trade."

That makes me laugh. "Not bad at all."

I stand, smoothing my skirts, suddenly restless.

Ready.

There's a knock at the door. "It's time," Duncan says from the hall.

Maisy gives me one last look, her eyes full of pride and love. "Go on, then. He's waiting."

I step out of my chamber, my hands trembling, my heart thumping so loud I'm sure Maisy can hear it from beside me. The corridor feels longer than it ever has. I clutch my flowers tightly, the lilacs in my hair filling the air with a magical scent as we walk.

I stop just outside the archway of the chapel.

"Breathe," Maisy whispers.

I try.

My gown is simple but lovingly made, soft green velvet with fine gold embroidery at the sleeves. I wear my mother's brooch with the Lennox crest pinned just above my heart, and beneath my skirt, hidden from view, my father's dagger, the MacRae crest etched into the hilt. I carry both of them with me as I step forward into what comes next.

The strings start playing, strong and clear, and I know it's time. Rory chose this song—*Maybe I'm Amazed*. He hummed it for the musicians so they could learn it for our special day, saying it reminded him of home, and of me.

I walk in alone.

In the chapel, all heads turn, but I barely see them. I only see Rory, standing at the far end, his eyes locked on mine like I'm the only thing in the world that matters.

He's dressed in a fresh tunic and the MacRae plaid draped over his shoulder, a silver clasp at his collar. There's a sureness in his smile, but behind it, I can see the awe in his face, like he can't believe I'm his.

And I can't believe he's mine.

Rory meets me halfway, and we turn together to face the altar. Duncan steps forward. Today, he's not just my brother. He's a laird, witness, and the one giving me away.

We offer our vows the old way, hands clasped.

"I vow to stand with you in every season," I say, my voice clear. "In peace and in war, in joy and in sorrow, I will not walk ahead or behind, but beside you."

Rory's hands are warm around mine. "I vow to honor your strength and your fire, and to protect you while giving you a haven where you can be soft, whenever you need to be. You are my home, Cait, and I am yours."

The priest blesses our union in Gaelic, his voice low and melodic. Duncan wraps the ceremonial cloth around our joined hands, the plaid of our clan binding us in blood and promise. Then he nods to us.

"You may kiss your wife."

Rory lifts my hands and presses a kiss to my knuckles, then leans in and brushes his lips to mine.

The chapel erupts in loud cheers—clapping, whistles, laughter. I hear Maisy crying, and someone—probably Tavish—yelling, "About time!" But none of it touches me.

All I feel is Rory's arms around me, and the steadiness of his breath as he holds me like he never intends to let go.

I never thought I'd marry for love, and I certainly never thought love would look like this: a time traveler and a laird's daughter. A beginning shaped by the magic of the river, but forged in battle.

We walk down the aisle together, hand in hand, our hearts aligned.

Outside, the sunshine is waiting, and the whole castle is alive with celebration. Music, clapping, the smell of venison roasting and bannocks baking. There will be dancing and toasts and hopefully too much wine.

But right now, as Rory lifts me up in his arms and spins me once, laughing into my hair, I know one thing for certain. Whatever storm comes next, I will face it with him. I will face it as his wife, and I've never felt more ready.

The great hall is unrecognizable. Candlelight glows in every corner, hundreds of flames flickering against the stone walls and polished wood. Garlands of pine, rosemary, and marsh orchid blooms drape from the beams above, their fragrances mingling with the scent of roasting meats and honeyed pastries.

Every table gleams with polished silver and the MacRae motto, *With Fortitude,* is stitched into every banner, and every ribbon. This is no ordinary feast, but the most elegant celebration.

Rory and I enter to the sound of cheers and pipes. My cheeks are already sore from smiling, but I can't stop. His hand at the small of my back, steadying me as we weave through the crowd, I hear my name called in every direction. My cousins, elders, warriors, the kitchen maids, and even little Gavin and Hamish shout their congratulations.

I glance up at Rory and find him staring at everything in stunned wonder. "Didn't think a sixteenth-century castle could pull this off, did you?" I tease. "There are no jumbotrons or roller coasters, but hopefully it's up to your standards."

He laughs. "It's perfect, and so much better than I ever expected."

We take our seats at the head table, food already arriving: venison glazed with wine and juniper, platters of spiced root vegetables, cheese wrapped in herbs, and barley cakes drizzled with honey.

And the wine—Saints above, the wine. Rich, dark, and smooth as silk. The best in the cellar, it tastes like it was bottled with magic.

"You're going to ruin me," Rory murmurs after his first sip. "How am I supposed to go back to drinking anything else?"

"You're not," I grin, raising my cup to his. "You live here now."

The toasts begin. Duncan stands first, raising his goblet and speaking with a voice steadier than I expected.

"To my sister, the fiercest woman I know. And to Rory, who somehow managed to win her heart and all of ours in the process. May your days be full of laughter, your nights full of peace, and your home always be strong, even when the world is not."

We raise our cups and drink. The wine warms me all the way down. One by one, others stand to offer heartfelt blessings.

Then the music begins, and Rory and I dance for the first time as husband and wife. At first, I try to guide him through the steps, but Rory surprises me. He's clumsy at times, yes, but such a quick learner. He laughs as he spins me, just slightly off rhythm, but with such joy that I don't care at all. I forget every practiced step and just move.

He lifts me once, effortlessly, and I throw my head back and laugh. The entire hall is dancing now, boots thudding, skirts swirling, children darting under tables.

The tempo slows, a quieter song rises from the lute and fiddle, a melody so hauntingly beautiful it makes my throat ache.

Rory takes both my hands and pulls me close. We sway, slow and easy, and the rest of the world blurs into candlelight and shadows. I close my eyes and let myself feel everything. The music, his arms around me, the weight of the ring on my finger, the warmth of wine in my cheeks and chest, the peace and contentment in my soul.

"I never imagined a night like this," he whispers.

"Neither did I," I murmur back.

When the music fades and the laughter softens, when skirts rustle and chairs scrape as guests slip off to their chambers and the fire burns low, Rory laces his fingers through mine. Together, we walk down the quiet corridor toward my—no, our—room.

The door creaks open. Inside, the hearth glows low and golden, casting flickers of light across the bed. A mountain of furs and fresh linens, dusted with wildflower petals. Maisy's been in here preparing, which makes my chest ache in the best way.

I close the door behind us. For a long moment, neither of us moves.

Then Rory steps closer. "I'll never forget how beautiful you looked today, as long as I live," he says quietly.

I reach up and brush a curl from his brow. "You look so handsome, I thought I would never catch my breath."

My hands find the ties of his tunic. His fingers fumble with the laces at the back of my gown. We move clumsily, a little unsteady with wine and nerves, laughing when a knot won't budge or a sleeve turns inside out.

I step out of my wedding dress, the cool air skimming across my skin, and Rory inhales sharply.

"You are…." His voice trails off.

"Still me," I whisper, taking his hand and guiding it to my heart. "Just me."

"Gorgeous," he whispers.

We fall into the bed together, the furs warm beneath us. His body fits against mine like he was shaped just to hold me. I trace the line of his jaw, the scar across his ribs, the solid and strong lines of his muscles, carved by something divine.

Outside, the wind rattles the shutters. Inside, there's only the hush of breath and the thump of two hearts finding a rhythm.

He kisses me, and I let myself melt into him.

"I love you," I whisper, afraid to say it too loud, like it might startle the magic away.

He kisses the corner of my mouth. "You're the best thing that's ever happened to me."

Rory's lips trail along my collarbone and down to my breasts. He toys with me, causing me to lose control. My body writhes under the light teasing of his tongue on my nipples, and the pressure of his finger against my most sensitive area.

He throbs in my hand as I stroke. I need to feel him inside of me. "Please, Rory?" I whisper.

He enters me slowly, and I gasp at the intensely sensual feeling. We move together, gently at first, then with more urgency. His eyes stay on mine like he's trying to memorize the way this feels. Our hands grip together tightly when we finally reach the peak together, and it's like time stands still, just for a moment.

Later, when the fire is little more than a smolder and the petals are crushed beneath us, we lie tangled in the blankets, my head on his chest. As he pulls sprigs of lilac from my hair I whisper, "I'm so happy you stayed here, with me, in this time."

I feel it deep inside. We're meant to be.

CHAPTER 28

The fire's nearly out, the air cool enough now that Cait shifts closer in her sleep, one leg sliding over mine beneath the blanket. Her breath is slow and even, her head tucked beneath my chin. The last of the flower petals are crushed, and I still smell them in her hair.

I've never felt anything like this contentment. I close my eyes and tighten my arm around her waist as if I can hold the moment still.

Then I hear it.

A clang, like metal on stone.

I snap my eyes open. Cait stirs, murmuring something unintelligible in her sleep. I lift my head, straining to hear outside the castle walls.

Another sound—closer this time. A door slamming. A muffled yell. Not the drunken laughter from earlier. No, this sound carries urgency.

"Cait," I whisper, shaking her gently. "Wake up."

She blinks at me, confused, still half in dreams. "What—?"

"We're not alone."

There's a crash below us, glass, or pottery, followed by the sharp ring of steel. Cait bolts upright. We're both naked, but there's no time for modesty. I leap from the bed, grab my trousers and tunic, and throw Cait her shift.

The door bursts open and Duncan barrels in, barefoot, his hair wild, eyes furious. "The MacIntyres are inside the walls."

Cait gasps.

"They breached the outer gate. Must've used the distraction of the wedding to slip in. Gave the guards outside too much or too toxic a drink, and they're asleep in the tents."

"They poisoned the guards?" My blood runs cold.

Duncan tosses me a sword, and we follow him down the corridor, the stone freezing cold under our feet. As we pass the stairwell, I see them—MacIntyre men flooding through the main hall, axes in hand, cloaks dark and faces twisted in rage.

They're not here to make demands. They're here to kill us.

Duncan calls for the castle guard, but it's chaos. Half of them are still disoriented, drunk from the celebration. We race past a tapestry as it goes up in flames, ignited by a torch thrown by one of our attackers.

A scream echoes from the great hall—followed by another crash. I don't know who's winning or how many more are still outside.

We reach the kitchen, breathless, just as two MacIntyre brutes come crashing through the servants' entrance. Duncan meets them head-on with a roar, swinging his blade with brutal efficiency. Cait throws a knife—her father's—and it lodges in the throat of the second man before he can raise his axe.

He falls with a gurgle.

Cait retrieves her blade, her face pale, but steady. She turns to me, breath ragged. "We hold the castle," she says.

"Together," I reply.

We sprint for the great hall, and the doors are wide open, I taste the iron tang of blood and nearly choke on it. This was our wedding hall just hours ago, glowing with candlelight, echoing with music, and now, it's a battlefield.

The garlands that once hung from the beams are trampled underfoot, and tables are overturned. One of the MacRae banners burns in the corner, flames licking up the embroidered motto—*With Fortitude.*

Cait doesn't hesitate. She launches herself into the fray, her dagger flashing as she knocks a MacIntyre fighter off balance. His inexperience costs him, she drives her blade clean into his side, and he collapses, groaning.

I fight beside her, parrying a strike, my sword sliding across a MacIntyre axe handle, sparks flying. He slams me backward, but I twist free and land a blow to his ribs that sends him sprawling.

Everywhere I look, the MacRaes are trying to rally, but we were caught unprepared, too drunk, too scattered. I see Duncan across the hall, his blade coated red, shouting orders, trying to form a line.

"Stop them!" he yells. "Push them out!"

But then I hear Cait cry out behind me.

I spin, my heart lurching, but she's already disappeared behind a wave of moving bodies. A group of MacIntyres charge through the broken doors, axes swinging, and she vanishes between them like a ghost.

"Cait!"

I shove forward, past limbs, screaming her name again. My voice is swallowed by the noise: steel on steel, wailing, the crash of furniture, the moan of the wounded.

She was just here.

I won't lose her. Not again. Not tonight.

A warrior comes at me with a spear—I sidestep and drive my blade up under his arm. He falls with a grunt, and I step over him, blood hot on my hands.

"Cait!" I call again, searching the sea of confusion for her.

Nothing.

A massive MacIntyre with a wild beard and chainmail comes at me roaring, swinging a broadsword like a battering ram. I barely get my blade up in time to block, the force jarring all the way down to my bones.

"Where is she?" I snarl, pushing back with everything I have.

He only grins. "The lass? Maybe she's dead already."

Rage erupts in me. I throw my whole weight into the next blow, slamming my pommel into his jaw. He stumbles, and I drive my sword into his stomach. His breath leaves him in a wheeze, and he crumples.

Where is she?

Another scream—not hers. A MacRae warrior is struck down near the musicians' platform. I recognize one of the fiddlers, lying still with blood across his face.

I scramble over a fallen bench, slipping on blood, trying to reach the hearth where Cait laughed when I tripped over my own feet during the dance. But she's not there.

She's not anywhere.

And the MacIntyres are still pouring in.

I hear Duncan calling my name, but it sounds far away. My heart's pounding too loud in my ears.

"Cait!" I scream again, raw and desperate now.

Still no answer.

I tighten my grip on my sword, the hilt slick with blood.

"Hold fast!" Duncan roars again from across the smoke-filled hall.

And I do.

I swing at the next MacIntyre I see. He blocks, but I'm faster. I catch his thigh, then his side, and he goes down hard. I don't look back.

Duncan reaches me, breathless and bloodied. His cheek is split open, and one sleeve is soaked red.

Our warriors, disheveled from drink and sleep, are starting to recover now, sobered by rage. The MacRaes are rallying, pushing back with blades, axes, and fists. From the far side of the room, I hear someone announce that the gate has been barred. The invaders are trapped.

I don't even see the blade until it's too late.

A MacIntyre comes out of the shadows to my left, a quick, dirty fighter, short sword in hand. I block his first strike but not the second. The tip of his blade slices across my side, deep enough to burn.

I grunt, stumbling back. The pain is white-hot, slicing through adrenaline and rage. My tunic darkens, warm and wet.

"Rory!" Duncan plunges his sword through the man who stabbed me, pulling it out as the bastard falls to the floor.

"Are ye hurt?"

"I'm fine," I lie, breath ragged. "Just a scratch."

He doesn't believe me, but he doesn't argue. There's no time.

We move as one. Shoulder to shoulder, we push toward the center of the hall. The enemy is breaking formation now—growing sloppy. Maybe they thought we'd fall easier. They were wrong.

I slash one down, another charges, and Duncan tackles him, driving him into an overturned bench before finishing him.

The smoke stings my eyes. Somewhere overhead, part of a timber groans and falls, sending a shower of sparks across the room.

More of our men pour in now, roused from the barracks, some of them half-dressed, still barefoot, but ready to fight. A cook has a bloodied frying pan in place of a shield.

It's enough.

We push them back, one step at a time, until the MacIntyres start to realize the trap they're in. They came through the front gates, and now those gates are closed. The windows are narrow. The castle is ours.

One man breaks and runs. Then another.

Duncan bellows, "Don't let them regroup! Cut them down!"

A dozen of our warriors give chase, and I follow, clutching my side, which is throbbing now, warm and pulsing. I feel dizzy, but I keep moving.

In the corridor, three MacIntyres try to escape through the servants' wing, but our men corner them. One drops his weapon and surrenders. The other two try to fight, but they don't make it far. Steel sings. Blood spatters the wall.

By the time we circle back to the hall, only a few stragglers remain. Two more try to bolt through the kitchens and are brought down by arrows. One leaps from a narrow window and lands badly, his scream cutting through the air before it ends in a sickening crunch.

And then it's over. The last clang of steel fades.

I stagger, suddenly unsteady. My legs won't hold. Duncan catches me just before I hit the floor and eases me down.

"Bloody fool," he mutters. "You're bleeding like a pig."

"Don't let them get away," I whisper, blinking hard. "Some ran."

"They won't get far. I'll see to it." He rips a strip from his already torn sleeve and presses it to my side, making me hiss in pain. "You need a damn healer."

"I need Cait."

His jaw tightens. "We'll find her."

He says it like a promise. Like he'll tear the castle apart stone by stone if he has to.

And I believe him.

But as I lie here, my breath coming fast, my body in agony, all I can see is that empty patch of floor where she vanished.

Gone.

And I don't know if she's alive.

CHAPTER 29

The great hall is too crowded, too violent—and I'm shoved back, stumbling through the narrow corridor. I clutch my dagger tightly, pressing my back to the cold wall, breathing hard.

The sounds of clashing steel and shouted orders seep through the thick stone, and my mind is on Maisy and her bairns. They were in their quarters, alone and unprotected, before the madness began. I dart down the hallway, praying they're safe. I can't leave them vulnerable now.

The door to Maisy's room is cracked, a thin sliver of light leaking out. I shove it open.

Her eyes are full of terror when she sees me. They're all alive. Her bairns cling to her skirts, crying and trembling.

"Cait, thank God," Maisy whispers, her voice shaking.

"I'm here," I say. "We need to get you and the bairns somewhere safe. Now."

Maisy nods, swallowing hard. She's dressed in a rough woolen nightgown, her body shaking in fear as she gathers her bairns closer. I realize I'm barely more armed than they are, my dagger the only weapon.

I move to barricade the door with a heavy chest, the wood scraping and thudding against the frame.

A sudden crash outside makes us all freeze. The enemy has found us.

"Get behind me," I command, my voice sharp.

The fear in their eyes stabs me deeper than any wound. The wood shudders under heavy blows. I draw my dagger with shaking fingers, grip tight as iron. My heart hammers in my chest, and I plant myself between Maisy, her bairns, and the splintering wood.

I glance back once. "Stay behind me. Don't move."

A final crash—the door bursts open, flying inward on broken hinges. Three MacIntyre men storm through, kicking the wooden chest into pieces. One brandishes a short sword. Another holds a rusted axe. The third has blood down his arm but moves fast, his teeth bared in a snarl, swinging his sword.

I step forward, lifting my dagger.

Then Maisy's voice cuts through the air, "Cait—take this!"

She slides something out from under her bed and across the floor. It clatters—Ewan's sword.

I drop to one knee, my fingers closing around the hilt. It's heavier than I expect, solid and sure, the weapon that carries Ewan's memory.

I rise.

The first man swings for me. I duck low, spinning beneath the arc of his sword, and slash out. My blade sings as it slices across his thigh. He stumbles, howling, and I don't stop. I drive the blade into his jaw, and he crashes to the floor.

The second rushes me with the axe. I sidestep, just barely missing the swing that would've cut me in two. His weight carries him past me, and I turn fast, driving Ewan's sword into his back with all the force I have. He falls hard and doesn't move again.

The last one lunges for Maisy.

"No!" I shout, throwing myself between them.

He grabs my arm, his fingers bruising, trying to twist the sword from my grip. I elbow him in the gut, wrench free, and kick him backward. He snarls, grabbing my braid and slicing it off, but I slash across his forearm. He shrieks and falls back against the wall. Without hesitation, I thrust my sword through his guts.

They're through.

The only sound is the ragged pant of my breath and the soft cries of Maisy's bairns. My whole body shakes now that the fight is over, and sweat stings my eyes.

Maisy rushes to me, "Cait—oh, God—"

"I'm fine," I rasp. "They're gone. For now."

She nods, blinking back tears. Leana starts to cry, and she scoops her up, cradling her close.

Maisy's voice breaks. "You saved us. I don't know how to thank you."

I lean my head out of the room, scanning the dark hallway beyond the broken door. "We're not done yet. There might be more coming."

Maisy shudders, holding her bairns tighter. "The castle—it's fallen?"

"Not yet," I murmur. "We need to move quickly."

I keep Ewan's sword in hand as we walk quietly. The halls beyond are silent for now.

One of the bairns, Kenna, with blue eyes and dark curls, reaches out and takes my free hand. Her grip is tiny but fierce.

I squeeze back, steeling myself. "This way," I say, glancing behind us. The hallway is dark and empty.

I slide my fingers along the wall until I find the hidden latch, and with a small creak, the narrow panel groans open. Cold air rushes out, damp and musty. I usher Maisy inside first, then help the bairns through the tight space, crouching to fit.

"They'll never think to look here," I whisper, bracing the panel halfway closed. "No one's used this tunnel in years. It leads to the old priest's quarters behind the chapel. Go all the way there and hide. Be silent. We will find you when it's safe."

The bairns sniffle but stay quiet, burying their faces in their mother's nightgown. Maisy's voice trembles. "What about you?"

"I have to find Rory and Duncan. And I have to make sure no more of those bastards are roaming the halls." I press the hilt of

Ewan's sword tighter in my grip. My side aches where a blade grazed me earlier, but I ignore it.

Maisy catches my hand. "Cait... come with us."

I shake my head. "Keep them safe. Stay quiet."

I push the panel shut before she can argue, sealing them in darkness, and hopefully, safety. Then I rise, sword in hand, moving cautiously through the dim hallways of the castle.

Bodies lie scattered—MacRaes and MacIntyres alike, some frozen in the final, desperate moments of battle, with shocked eyes, mouths frozen open as if still gasping for breath.

I search each room, calling his name softly at first, then with growing desperation.

"Rory," I whisper, my voice cracking.

No answer.

The great hall is a ruin. The torn banners hang limp and singed, the broken tables scattered like wreckage. I don't dare stay long. The eerie quiet presses down like a weight.

I pass the kitchen—no sign of him.

I descend the stairwell toward the cellar, the steps cold and slick beneath my bare feet. The air grows heavy with dampness and the faint smell of herbs. I hear familiar voices—low and urgent.

I hurry down the last few steps, my heart leaping.

Mairen is there, kneeling beside Rory, who lies sprawled against the rough stone wall. Duncan stands nearby, his sword sheathed but his expression tense.

Rory's face is pale, sweat clinging to his brow. His shirt is torn, revealing a deep, ragged wound on his side. Blood seeps through the cloth, dark and spreading.

"Rory!" I breathe, rushing to his side.

He turns his head slowly, a weary yet relieved smile touching his lips. "Cait...."

I drop to my knees, gripping his hand. "You're hurt bad."

He winces, closing his eyes briefly. "It's nothing. I'll live. I'm so glad you are safe, my love."

"I was worried about you," I say.

Turning to Mairen, I ask, "How bad is it?"

She shakes her head, focused and calm. "The blade cut deep, but I've staunched the bleeding. He'll need rest and time, but he will make it. Stubborn as a mule, isn't he?"

"In the best way," is my response.

Rory winces, and I brush a damp curl from his forehead. "Rest now," I murmur, soft but firm. "You need to be still, or you'll tear the wound open again."

He tries to sit up straighter anyway. "I'm fine!"

"No, you're not," I cut in, placing a hand gently on his chest. "But you're alive. And Duncan is too. And Mairen." My throat tightens, but I try not to let it show. "That's more than I hoped for when it all began."

He nods, his eyes finding mine.

I turn to Duncan, who stands guard at the foot of the stairs, sword still stained, his jaw set.

"Is the castle secure?"

"Aye," he says without hesitation. "It should be. The tide had turned when Rory and I came down here. Mairen was hiding in the cellar, clever lass. I had her tend to Rory's wound while I went back up to give orders. I have men going room by room now, checking for stragglers, but most of the bastards are either dead or fleeing."

"Good," I say, exhaling slowly. "Maisy and her bairns—they're safe. I got them hidden in the north wall passageway, just before the fighting reached us. They should be in the old priest's quarters by now."

Duncan gives me a long, measured look, then nods. "You did well, Cait. I'll go fetch them. They must be frightened to the marrow."

"Aye, but announce yourself gently before barging in, Duncan. The bairns are terrified."

Duncan nods, leaving us to attend to Maisy.

"Wait...." Rory tries to sit up again. "You're telling me there really *are* secret passageways?"

"Yes, and if you'll be still and rest, I'll show them to you one day," I reply, returning to his side.

Mairen glances at me and lifts an eyebrow, her lips curving into the beginnings of a smile. "Fought off raiders in nothing but your shift, did you? You're a fierce hero, lass. The songs will be scandalous."

I scoff under my breath, suddenly aware of the state I'm in—bare feet, smudged with soot, my shift torn and bloodied.

Rory stirs again and reaches for my hand. His fingers wrap loosely around mine, rough and warm despite the tremble. "You look beautiful," he says hoarsely. "I love your new hairstyle."

I blink. "Hair?" Then I remember—one of those MacIntyre clotpolls sliced my braid clean off.

My fingers drift to the back of my neck. Nothing but ragged ends of curls remain.

I laugh. "I forgot about my hair, and the shift."

Rory's lips twitch into a tired grin. "Unforgettable, actually."

I shake my head, still smiling. "Let's hope the bards leave *that* part out of the tale."

Mairen snorts. "Not a chance."

And despite the blood, the smoke, the pain—despite everything we've just survived—there's a sliver of hope in my chest. We may be bruised, bloody, and weary, but we're still breathing.

THE CASTLE FEELS QUIETER NOW, BUT THE SILENCE IS HEAVY WITH THE weight of the ambush. We were blessed enough to keep our home standing, with only certain areas of some rooms damaged by flames.

We will rebuild.

I move slowly through the corridors, my steps careful over uneven floors and splattered stains. The wounded lie in makeshift beds set up in every hall and chamber. Some sleep deeply, lulled by pain or exhaustion. Others cry softly, clutching broken limbs or fresh bandages.

Mairen and the other healers work tirelessly, moving between patients with gentle hands and fierce determination. They barely sleep, and I help them when I'm not tending to Rory.

The dead have been gathered. Soldiers and servants alike are laid out respectfully before being buried together in the hillside cemetery. Duncan led the somber task, reading prayers over the graves.

It wasn't just warriors who died. The servants who tried to defend themselves fell alongside the men-at-arms. Faces I'd seen every day, now only memories.

The great hall is cold, stripped of all festivity. Long wooden tables sit bare, save for scattered maps, parchments, and weapons laid out with careful purpose. Torches burn low along the stone walls, flickering shadows across faces etched with weariness and worry.

I stand near the center, Rory seated at my side, his strength not fully returned. Duncan stands just in front of us, ready to address the crowd.

The elders and chieftains gather around stoic men and women who have led their people through winters, famines, and wars.

The air hums with tension. This meeting isn't just about strategy. It's about survival. The future of our land rests on what we decide here.

Duncan clears his throat and steps forward, his voice steady but grave. "The scouts rode hard and far, covering every path the MacIntyres or Drummonds might use to strike again."

He pauses, letting the weight of his words settle. "What they found... is good. Both clans are battered nearly to breaking. Their numbers thinned by battle and internal strife."

One of the elder women, Ellen MacRae, narrows her eyes. "So they won't come again soon?"

"Not in force, no. The scouts reported only small bands—scattered survivors trying to regroup. They lack the strength to launch another major assault anytime soon."

I nod, adding, "But that doesn't mean the threat is gone. These clans are cunning and ruthless. They'll test our defenses when we least expect it. We should not have let our guards down for the wedding celebration. Next time we will be much better prepared."

A murmur ripples through the council.

Ellen MacRae speaks again, her voice softer now. "Aye. We must stay vigilant."

Duncan meets her gaze. "We're strengthening patrols along every border. The scouts have orders to watch for any signs of movement or plots. The men and women on the walls will not rest."

Rory gestures toward the maps spread on the long table. "We've marked the routes the MacIntyres and Drummonds have used in the past. We're reinforcing weak points with traps and hidden posts. Our archers are drilling harder than ever."

One of the older chieftains scratches his grizzled beard thoughtfully. "This council has stood for generations through peace and war alike. We've faced worse and endured. You all fought bravely to defend us. Your actions kept many alive."

A flush of pride warms me despite the exhaustion. Rory's jaw tightens in silent acknowledgment.

The chieftain's voice is solemn. "But it's more than strength of arms. We need unity, resolve. These clans seek to divide us, to weaken our bonds."

Ellen MacRae nods in agreement. "We must stand as one—MacRaes, Lennoxes, every household and clan within these lands."

Duncan's gaze hardens. "And we'll do it. We're planning training for every able-bodied soul. Everyone who can hold a blade or aim a bow will learn to defend what's ours."

Rory adds, "We're also repairing the castle's defenses. Walls and gates strengthened. We cannot afford to be caught unprepared again. This attack showed us our weaknesses, but it also revealed our strength—our courage and loyalty. We will rebuild. We will prepare. And if they come again, they will find us ready."

The elders nod slowly, acceptance settling over the room. Ellen MacRae's last words ring out clear and true: "Then let it be so. We are MacRae. We endure. We fight. Together."

Outside, the wind rustles the banners that still fly—tattered but unbowed.

With Fortitude.

CHAPTER 30

The morning sun crests over the hills, casting gold light across the charred stone walls of the great hall. Smoke hasn't clung to these stones in weeks, but I swear I can still smell it when the wind shifts just so.

Rory says it's in my head, and perhaps he's right.

Still, I can't help but glance at the beams where the worst of the fire raged. We've lifted fresh beams, and the stone masons have replaced many of the crumbled walls.

"We're getting there," Rory says beside me, his voice low and rough with sleep. He's leaning on his cane this morning, but he's up and moving, and that's more than I could have hoped for three months ago.

"You should be resting," I murmur, though I don't really mean it. I like having him beside me when we survey the damage and the progress. Although we've stopped calling it *damage* aloud. Now, we talk about what's next. What needs fixing up, and what must be made better than it was.

He raises an eyebrow. "You say that every morning. And yet, here I am."

I smile despite myself. His face is still drawn with pain some days, but his wit has come back in full force. He tugs gently at a strand of my hair. "And *you're* growing wild again."

"I look ridiculous," I mutter, swatting his hand away. "Like a hedge witch who got halfway through a curse and forgot what she was doing."

Rory's laugh echoes. When he catches his breath, he says, "I asked you not to make me laugh so hard. It still hurts. But you do look beautiful with your hair long or short, my love."

I roll my eyes, but it softens something in my chest. He's lying, of course. My hair's uneven where it was hacked off, tufts curling at odd angles, but it's coming back. Like everything else. Slowly. Stubbornly.

We step outside of the castle, greeting guards, gardeners, and others working in the courtyard.

Below the ridge, the clang of hammers and the grind of wagon wheels echo through the valley. The new watchtower is half-raised—three stories so far, with a ladder lashed to its frame and archers training in rotating shifts, which was Rory's idea.

Duncan has taken full charge of the military now, and for once, I don't question his authority. He moves through the ranks like a man born for it—stern but fair, and fiercely protective.

"Duncan's posted another five men along the southern perimeter," I say. "And the armory has nearly doubled. We'll be ready if they come again."

"We won't be caught in our honeymoon clothes next time," Rory says, his mouth tugging into a crooked grin.

I nudge him with my shoulder. "I like your honeymoon clothes."

Rory laughs again, so loudly he flinches from the pain in his side. "You are going to kill me, woman."

Three months ago, Rory was wounded so badly, I didn't know if he'd live. I didn't know if I could live without him. Now, the two of us are at the helm of something larger than revenge or survival. We're building a place where people are safe. Where they *belong*.

Heading down the hill slowly, with Rory keeping pace without complaint, we see bairns hauling buckets of mortar and passing them to the builders. A lass no older than ten gives us a gap-toothed smile as she hands off her load.

"You're doing the work of five men," I call out, and she beams.

"It's going to be beautiful, Lady Cait," she says, wiping sweat from her brow. "Even better than before."

A lump rises in my throat. "Aye. It will."

Together, we walk into the heart of it all, the ashes and the stone, the noise and the hope, and we begin again. Now it's all ours to carry. The tenants in the village, the cooks and stable boys, the old women who stitch blankets in the north wing, the children who lost fathers in the fire–they look to us not for miracles, but for stability. For proof that the world didn't end that night.

Sometimes, that means helping with planting. Sometimes, it's just standing there while they talk about a broken cartwheel, a sick goat, or night terrors they can't shake.

We walk the grounds together, Rory and I, stopping at the orchard wall where the painter's apprentice has been restoring the mural of the harvest goddess. She bows when we approach, a smear of red paint on her cheek.

"How's the repair?" I ask.

"Almost done, my lady. The lower section was blackened, but I'm matching pigments."

I study her work—bright gold, crimson, and orange against old stone. "She's beautiful."

"She's hope," the lass says softly.

I nod and leave a coin on the ledge beneath the mural.

By midday, the castle is noisy with labor and laughter. Maisy's bairns chase their dog through the corridors. A baker curses in delight when his loaves rise just right. I hear music again, fife and fiddle, and it almost makes me cry. Not because it's sad, but because it means we're all alive.

In the great hall, the long tables have been rejoined, the soot scraped from the stonework. They'll be filled again soon.

Rory moves behind me, wraps his arms around my waist, and presses his chin to my shoulder. "The people trust you."

"I'm not sure I've earned it."

"You're still here. We held the castle. That earns more than you think."

Soon, there will be another meeting. There are land boundaries to redraw, wounded soldiers needing reassignment. But for one heartbeat, I let myself lean back against him, let myself feel the comfort of arms that hold without hesitation.

We're tired and still healing, but we listen, we rebuild, we care, and that, somehow, is enough.

IT'S LATE, AND THE CASTLE IS QUIET NOW, SAVE FOR THE SOFT WHISPERS of the wind against the windows. Outside, the last remnants of the day's heat linger in the stone, but inside, the room is cool and calm, wrapped in the deep hush of evening.

I sit on the edge of the bed, my legs folded beneath me, my back to the fire. I watch Rory undress, the lines of his incredibly chiseled body causing butterflies to rise within me.

Tonight, there are no wounds to tend to, no whispers of danger. The castle feels peaceful, and I want to hold onto it for as long as I can.

Rory steps closer, his bare chest warm under the firelight, and I feel the pull of him, the gravity that draws me in. He's never once made me feel anything less than cherished. I feel it in the way he watches me when I'm lost in thought, the way his hands linger on me even in the simplest touches.

His fingers brush the back of my neck, sending a soft shiver down my spine, and I close my eyes at the touch.

"You're so beautiful," he says quietly, and the sincerity in his voice makes my chest ache.

The intensity in his gaze is something I've come to understand— it's the kind of look he gives me when he wants to see every part of me. Not just my body, but everything I am. The scars, the bruises, the pain of what we've survived, and the serenity of knowing I'm his.

"You make me feel that way," I reply, my voice low.

"I always will."

He steps closer, his hands now framing my face, and I melt into him as he bends to kiss me. It's soft, tender at first—gentle lips that speak a thousand unspoken things. His hand moves to my shoulder, brushing the strap of my nightgown aside, and I let him, feeling the cool air on my skin where the fabric falls away.

I lean into him, wrapping my arms around his neck, and pulling him closer. There's nothing rushed about it, just the slow, deliberate giving of ourselves to each other. His lips trail along my jaw, down my neck, and I feel the heat of his breath, the press of his body against mine.

I lean into him, feeling his muscles under my hands. He lays me back on the bed, his body against mine.

He traces the line of my jaw, my lips, before kissing me again, deeper this time, pulling a soft gasp from me as his hands slide along the curve of my waist.

"Do you ever wonder," he whispers, his voice rough, "how we got here? How we made it through all of it?"

"I think about it every day," I admit. "But... here. Now. I don't want to think about anything but this."

His lips curve into that smile, and he moves with me as if every curve of my body is already familiar to him. I lose myself in the way he touches me—slow, purposeful, yet with a fire that burns just beneath the surface. Every caress, every kiss, is a promise that he's still here, still mine, and I am still his. Even in the silence between us, there's a language only we speak.

His hand moves to my thigh, lifting my leg over his, and I arch into him instinctively, feeling the press of him, the heat of him. I cling to him, needing this closeness, this intimacy. There are no words needed now, only the connection that runs deeper than anything we've been through. The trust we've built, piece by piece.

When we come together, it's not just the physical pleasure, but the emotional closeness—the sense of safety that we've fought for and earned, that makes it sacred. We're not just lovers, we're survivors, partners, and, in this room, we are whole again.

I can't remember the last time I felt so at peace, so full, and I know that whatever storms come, we will face them together.

CHAPTER 31

Rory

The sky is the clearest shade of blue I've seen in months, like it's been scrubbed clean after all the fires, battles, death, and storms. I stand on the ridge just above the castle and look down at everything we've rebuilt.

The watchtower is finished, and the walls are reinforced. The courtyard is buzzing with life again: carts creaking, bairns laughing, the smith's hammer ringing out in steady rhythm. I breathe it all in and feel... peace.

Behind me, the wind stirs the heather, and below, the flag bearing Cait's family crest flies high and proud above the gate. Now, it's my crest and gate too. This is no longer just a place I landed by accident, or just a crumbling castle I helped put back together. It's home.

I shift my weight slightly, still favoring the side where the blade went in. The pain is a dull ache now, more memory than wound.

Every morning when I wake up next to Cait, tangled in wool blankets and firelight, I know I'm where I belong. I never expected to meet a woman like Cait. She's wild, sharp, stubborn... and when I look at her, I know I made the right choice.

"Rory!" a voice calls from below.

It's Duncan, already halfway up the slope toward me, his boots kicking up dirt. He's grown into the role of commander well. He always had the gumption for it, even if he used to hide it behind grins and jokes.

"We've started the drills," he says as he reaches me.

I give him a lazy salute, indicating I'll be there to help oversee the training session momentarily.

While I still help show the lads new fighting tactics and proper technique, I am usually found elsewhere. Cait and I run most of the castle now. She deals with supply ledgers, tenant disputes, and the finer points of diplomacy. I handle the blacksmith's orders, military rotation, and teaching the lads how to fire a longbow properly. We host feasts, resolve land claims, and listen to complaints about goats and grain stores.

It's nothing like the life I knew in the 21st century, but I've never been more useful or felt more loved.

After military drills, I look for Cait, finding her in the solar, standing by the window with a cup of tea in her hands. Her hair's longer now, brushing her shoulders in soft curls. She's humming under her breath, a little tune I don't recognize, and the light paints her in honey gold and copper.

We both still have battle scars, but they don't feel like marks of loss anymore. They're reminders of what we came through, and what we built afterward.

She takes my hand and leads me to the window seat. We sit together, watching the courtyard bustle below. The painter's apprentice is nearly finished with the mural of the harvest goddess, and I notice it resembles Cait.

"There's something I've been meaning to tell you," Cait says, her tone quieter now.

I glance over. She's fiddling with the edge of her sleeve, and seems nervous, which is unlike her.

"What is it?"

She takes a breath, then looks up at me, her eyes shining. "I'm carrying a bairn."

For a moment, the world stops.

I blink, sure I've misheard, but her face says everything.

"You—Cait—" My voice breaks. I swallow. "We're having a baby?"

She blushes and nods. "Aye."

I laugh, a sound that feels too big for my chest, and then I kiss her.

When we finally pull apart, I rest my hand over her belly, still flat beneath the wool of her dress.

"You've just made me the happiest man alive," I whisper.

She grins.

The rest of the day passes in a warm blur. We tell Maisy our good news, and her reaction makes me think she might be even more excited about our baby than we are.

Duncan pretends to groan, but then he slips me a flask and deadpan calls me "Da," which makes me laugh so hard I can't breathe.

We sit by the fire later, just the two of us. Cait leans into my side, and I run my fingers through her hair, thinking about how far we've come. The woman who stood beside me in fire and blood. The one carrying our future.

I could've gone back to the internet, electricity, and running water, but none of it held a candle to this—to her.

Cait shifts, her hand finding mine beneath the blanket. "What are you thinking about?" she murmurs.

"You," I say. "Us. The life we chose."

She hums. "I used to think I'd marry Lachlan, live out my days in quiet obligation. Never really love. Never really be seen."

I tilt her chin to look at me. "You are seen. Every inch of you. Every laugh and scar and sigh. You're my whole world, Cait."

She kisses me, slow and certain. "And you're mine."

Outside, a storm rolls in, tapping against the windows, but inside our chamber, there's only warmth and soft light. We sit like that until the fire goes low and the castle quiets.

In the darkness, I feel the thrum of life—hers, mine, the tiny one growing inside her—and I know without a doubt that I made the right choice.

This is our home, our family, and our time.

194

Thank you for reading! Back to Port Royal *is now available here!*

ALSO BY ID JOHNSON

Stand Alone Titles

<u>All I Want for Christmas is Pooch</u>

(*sweet contemporary romance*)

<u>Christmas Memory</u>

(*sweet contemporary romance*)

<u>The Doll Maker's Daughter at Christmas</u>

(*clean romance/historical*)

<u>Pretty Little Monster</u>

(*young adult/suspense*)

<u>The Journey to Normal: Our Family's Life with Autism</u> (*nonfiction*)

<u>Found by the Alpha (fantasy romance)</u>

Love Throughout Time

(*time travel romance*)

Back to Titanic

Back to Gettysburg

Back to Bunker Hill

Back to the Highlands

Back to Port Royal

Back to the Spanish Inquisition (coming Sept 2025)

Silverwood Academy

(*paranormal romance*)

Vampire Hunter

World Builder

Realm Jumper

Celestial Springs

(psychological thriller/literary fiction/women's fiction)

Beneath the Inconstant Moon

The First Mrs. Edwards

Leaving Ginny

The Motherhood

(dystopian romance)

Rain's Rebellion

Rain's Run

Rain's Return

Ashes and Rose Petals

(contemporary romance/retelling of Romeo and Juliet and Cinderella)

Girl in the Attic

Girl From the Tomb

Girl On the Beach

Nashville Country Dreams

(contemporary romance)

Meant to Marry Me

Lead Me Home

You Are the Reason

Forever Love series

(clean romance/historical)

Cordia's Will: A Civil War Story of Love and Loss

Cordia's Hope: A Story of Love on the Frontier

The Clandestine Saga series

(paranormal romance)

<u>Transformation</u>

<u>Resurrection</u>

<u>Repercussion</u>

<u>Absolution</u>

<u>Illumination</u>

<u>Destruction</u>

<u>Annihilation</u>

<u>Obliteration</u>

<u>Termination</u>

A Vampire Hunter's Tale (based on The Clandestine Saga)

(paranormal/alternate history)

<u>Aaron</u>

<u>Jamie</u>

<u>Elliott</u>

<u>Christian</u>

The Chronicles of Cassidy (based on The Clandestine Saga)

(young adult paranormal)

<u>So You Think Your Sister's a Vampire Hunter?</u>

<u>Who Wants to Be a Vampire Hunter?</u>

<u>How Not to Be a Vampire Hunter</u>

<u>My Life As a Teenage Vampire Hunter</u>

<u>Vampire Hunting Isn't for Morons</u>

<u>Vampires Bite and Other Life Lessons</u>

<u>Gone Guardian</u>

<u>Death Does Not Become Her</u>

Blood of the Vampire Hunter (based on The Clandestine Saga)

(paranormal romance)

<u>Night Slayer</u>

<u>Shadow Stalker</u>

<u>Queen Catcher</u>

<u>Mother Hunter</u>

<u>Father Finder</u>

Ghosts of Southampton series

(historical romance)

<u>Prelude</u>

<u>Titanic</u>

<u>Residuum</u>

<u>Lusitania</u>

Heartwarming Holidays Sweet Romance series

(Christian/clean romance)

<u>Melody's Christmas</u>

<u>Christmas Cocoa</u>

<u>Winter Woods</u>

<u>Waiting On Love</u>

<u>Shamrock Hearts</u>

<u>A Blossoming Spring Romance</u>

<u>Firecracker!</u>

<u>Falling in Love</u>

<u>Thankful for You</u>

<u>Melody's Christmas Wedding</u>

<u>The New Year's Date</u>

Charles Town Brides (based on Heartwarming Holidays Sweet Romance)

(Christian/clean romance)

<u>From This Moment</u>

<u>Can't Help Falling in Love</u>

<u>It's Your Love</u>

<u>When You Say Nothing At All</u>

<u>My Girl</u>

<u>Unchained Melody</u>

<u>I Only Have Eyes For You</u>

<u>At Last</u>

<u>The Very Thought of You</u>

Reaper's Hollow

(paranormal/urban fantasy)

<u>Ruin's Lot</u>

<u>Ruin's Promise</u>

<u>Ruin's Legacy</u>

When Kings Collide

(steamy historical romance)

<u>Princess of Silence</u>

<u>Princess of Hearts</u>

Collections

<u>Ghosts of Southampton Books 0-2</u>

<u>Reaper's Hollow Books 1-3</u>

<u>The Clandestine Saga Books 1-3</u>

<u>The Chronicles of Cassidy Books 1-4</u>

<u>Celestial Springs Collection</u>

<u>Heartwarming Holidays Sweet Romance Books 1-3</u>

<u>Heartwarming Holidays Sweet Romance Books 4-7</u>

Websites: https://books2read.com/ap/xX7ZD8/ID-Johnson

For updates, visit www.authoridjohnson.blogspot.com

Follow on Twitter @authoridjohnson

Find me on Facebook at www.facebook.com/IDJohnsonAuthor

Instagram: @authoridjohnson

Follow me on Bookbub: https://www.bookbub.com/authors/id-johnson

www.ingramcontent.com/pod-product-compliance
Lightning Source LLC
Chambersburg PA
CBHW060318310726
48976CB00007B/2370